Praise for Martin Malone

'With its themes of incest, suicide, and general, horrible dysfunction, at times *Us* resembles a less-sickening version of Iain Banks' *The Wasp Factory* – there's a similarity of tone, that mixture of true nastiness and black humour. But this is ultimately a distinctly Irish book – and a very good one too. Anyone interested in discovering the mundane yet freakish realities of Ireland today (albeit as seen through a very dark filter) should read it' – *Irish American Post*

'Martin Malone writers stories of profound originality. He has a great sense of history and how it can be made special for a modern reader. His work searches out the spirit and language of many countries, and it is enticing from the first sentence … a writer to watch' – *Stand UK*

'This is a vital and readable book which highlights once again the guilt and denial endemic in our society' – *Evening Herald*

'Powerful, disturbing and profoundly moving' – *The Good Book Guide*

'A human story told with real emotion and sensitivity … Malone brings this story to life with an insight and understanding as only one who has been there can … an excellent read' – *Morning Star, UK*

'A traditional Irish story with occasional stunning images' – *The Irish Times*

'Extraordinarily accomplished and beautifully realised' – *Irish Examiner*

'There are no corny lines here – Malone's humour being of the pitch black variety' – *Sunday Tribune*

Also by Martin Malone

Novels
Valley of the Peacock Angel
The Only Glow of the Day
The Silence of the Glasshouse
The Broken Cedar (*IMPAC nominated*)
After Kafra

Short Stories
The Mango War & Other Stories
Deadly Confederacies

Radio Plays
The Devil's Garden
Song of the Small Bird
Rosanna Nightwalker

Stage
Rosanna Nightwalker

Non-Fiction
The Lebanon Diaries

About the Author

Martin Malone is an Irish novelist and short story writer. His novel *The Broken Cedar* was nominated for the 2003 International IMPAC Dublin Literary Award. *Us* won the John B. Keane/*Sunday Independent* Award and his short story collection, *The Mango War*, won the RTÉ Francis MacManus Award in 2004. Martin's work has also won the Killarney International Short Story Prize and was twice shortlisted for a Hennessy Award and a P. J. O'Connor Award. Martin also worked as a military policeman with the Irish Army, under the flag of the United Nations. He served five tours of duty in Lebanon and one in Iraq.

Martin Malone

Us

NEW ISLAND

US

First published by Poolbeg Press Ltd. 2000.

This edition published 2015
by New Island Books,
16 Priory Office Park,
Stillorgan,
Co. Dublin.

www.newisland.ie

PRINT ISBN: 978-1-84840-433-5
EPUB ISBN: 978-1-84840-434-2
MOBI ISBN: 978-1-84840-435-9

Typeset by JVR Creative India
Cover design by Mariel Deegan
Printed by Essentra

New Island received financial assistance from The Arts Council (*An Chomhairle Ealaíon*), 70 Merrion Square, Dublin 2, Ireland.

10 9 8 7 6 5 4 3 2 1

'You can lie without saying a word; you can lie without opening your lips; you can lie by silence.'

– John B. Keane

1

Morris

March

An unusual family. Us. There's Dad who isn't here but whose shadow is, and Mum who is here but whose heart is broken. There's Gina who's sad, and Karen who's not. There's Victor who's intelligent, and me who isn't. There was Adam, too, who hurt us more than we imagined we could be hurt.

We live in a large bungalow set in a corner of a field, near a crossroads. Dad farmed sheep and trained two racehorses. He did neither very well. We survived on what he made from selling off bits of the land and what he won from gambling. He is lucky at the horses. Back then, he only told us about his lucky days. He didn't have to mention his bad ones, we knew by the puss of him, the way his eyes squinted, as though he were trying to squeeze piss out of them.

Mum tends to her face a lot. Fighting wrinkle advancement on every front with all sorts of creams. She's losing the battle around her eyes, where the lines are deep. Dad used to tell her she could no sooner push back time than he could his belly-button. Mum didn't speak with him all that much. I think she blamed him for the lines about her eyes. Mum and Dad acted like people who were extremely fed up with each other and didn't know what to do about it. Dad is very small in Mum's eyes and has been for a long time. We didn't think he could get any smaller. But he did. This is how.

Mum has two friends who drop in a lot. She met Father Pat Toner through her best friend, Kay Walsh. They hold private meetings in the sitting-room, smoking, all crossing their legs as though they were afraid of farting in each other's company.

Victor says they talk a lot of shit about shit. I know they cross their legs because I brought in tea on a tray, and they all went quiet and said thanks very much. And they all had their legs crossed. It looked funny. It just did. I don't know why. Mum used to do that sometimes. Let off. We could be eating our dinner or anything. She blamed her stomach instead of her arse. Dad said she's full of wind. When Dad found something he didn't like about Mum, he sunk his teeth into it like a dog with a fresh bone. Anyway, Mum got the problem sorted out, so she doesn't get embarrassed in front of us any more. Sometimes I wonder where all her wind goes. We didn't mind her farting as much as we minded Dad for getting on to her. Nerves – I think Mum's stomach nerves were shot for a while, shot from worrying, but now she's sharing her worries with her friends, and I don't hear them farting, so they must be able to handle the pressure.

A week leading up to what happened Adam, Gina told us all she was pregnant. She's a very attractive redhead with a smooth figure. She wasn't happy with her breasts, though, because I'd caught her a couple of times feeling herself in the mirror, and sighing this way and that, as if she were half-afraid of discovering something. I heard her telling Karen she'd go absolutely fucking crazy if she ever found a hair growing around her nipple. But I think she's afraid of discovering something else now. Aunt Julie died before Christmas. And how she died affected all the women in our house something dreadful. Mum drove over to Doc Fleming in Kildare and got him to examine the lot of them. He booked them into a Dublin hospital for check-ups. Lately, Doc Fleming sends all his doubts to hospital. His confidence was shook when eight of his patients died in one week. Victor and me call him Doctor Doom, but not in front of the women.

Mum's about the worst affected. Aunt Julie's her sister. And they looked alike. She told Dad it was like looking at herself lying in the coffin. Of course, Dad had no drink in him, so he said nothing, just sat there in his armchair by the range, smoking his pipe. Probably wishing that it was Mum. Wishing with his eyes like he does with the horses he backs, wishing so hard it's not wishing but praying.

After Gina told the lot of us she was pregnant, none of us could say anything. A guy on the news talked about English soccer fans going mad on the streets in Holland. Dad's eyes went like grey slivers of steel. His cheeks went in, as though his heart had pulled on strings attached to them. Mum often said his heart was like a cactus, dry and spiky. We'd been eating our dinner. Mum puts a big effort into cooking the main evening meal. It's the one meal she insists we're all together for, in at the table, like a proper family. Once she tried to get us to say the Rosary, but praying together to stay together didn't sit easy with us, not with Dad about. Victor told me that God had put all the Antichrists under the one roof and surrounded them with a moat of sheepshite.

We sat like zombies around the table. Mum's hands were on her throat, checking to see that she hadn't said *she* was pregnant. Karen's eyes fell sleepy. She'd known, of course. No one can sneeze in this house without her knowing. But she didn't know everything. I found out she didn't later, when we got closer and didn't pick on each other all the time. We thought Dad would lose his temper. Sometimes he does over nothing. He'd be so quiet in himself, and then he'd get thick about something: the TV being too loud, someone leaving a smell in the loo, one of us lazy about getting out of bed, stuff like that. *Pregnant.* Jesus.

Mum's hands shot to her temples. Karen buried a nervous smile. Victor looked up from his book. He's always reading, even at the table; he says his nerves can't stand people making slopping noises. Adam had tracks on his teeth, so he probably made the most noise. He asked Victor what he wanted him to do – shove his food up his butt? Adam could be crude. Victor's reading *Robinson Crusoe*. Must be for the fortieth time. He loves the idea of being away on a desert island, away from everyone. Though he says he'd have a preference for a Woman Friday. He thinks the author might have been a little queer to think up a Man Friday in the first place. Though the times he lived in might have had some bearing on his decision. They liked to keep the lid on their shit back then. Legs crossed, maybe?

Victor and me are twins. I'm thirteen years, four months and three days old. He's two minutes older. He says on the way out he grabbed the only brains on offer. Karen says he grabbed the good looks too. She said that to spite me. But Victor is handsome. He has jet-black hair, lean features and large blue eyes you'd think a clear sky had spat into. My hair isn't so dark, features aren't so lean. My nose – well – Victor says whoever had it last time must have been a boxer ... who jabbed with his snout.

Dad and Adam stared at each other. Gina stared at the two of them, then the rest of us.

Adam had his own room. He used to hand his shoes down to Dad. Mum blames the chemicals in the food chain for the kids being so tall these days; 'big-feeted kids,' she says, when she's full of Bailey's. Talking about Adam's yacht-sized footwear parked on the hairmat.

He never put away his shoes in the shoe cabinet Mum bought in Argos in Tallaght. She was always getting on to him about it. He never listened. He ignored her sometimes, just to annoy her.

'Pregnant!' Mum's shriek pierced my thoughts.

Gina bit her lower lip.

'How … who … you stupid little bitch. How could you be so stupid?'

Tears came to Gina's eyes. Genuine, I'm sure. My sisters can do that: turn tears on and off at will.

'Who?' Mum demanded.

She wanted to know who so she could kill him. She couldn't kill Gina, although part of her probably wanted to. Victor told me afterwards that some women blame men for getting them pregnant without realising they had something to do with it too. It proved, he said, how easily women can forget things when they want.

'Terry,' Gina said.

She said Terry as if the lot of us should know him.

A certain colour came to Adam's cheeks. More purplish than red. His eyebrows moved up and down. He was seventeen. His face had fiery red pimples and his lips were thin as razor-blade edges. He'd light fairish hair which he kept smoothing and it was always gelled. Sometimes he put dyes in his fringe: blue and pink. He loved watching the wrestling on TV. His favourite wrestler was 'The Undertaker'. I didn't like it so much at the start, but I like it now. Adam used to practise his moves on me and Victor but Victor used to get so serious. He punched Adam on the nose and drew blood that pumped like it was never going to stop. Adam didn't go crazy. He just paled. That finished the wrestling messing for us – Mum went spare. Victor said Adam had him pinned, what else could he do? Adam said Victor didn't like being bested by anyone.

Dad hated the sport, said nancy boys played it, and that the whole thing was just a rig-up. We thought he was so anti-wrestling because it was Adam's hobby. And Adam thought so too.

Dad jumped to his feet, his eyes full of storms. Looking at us as though we were to blame for Gina getting herself pregnant.

'Terry who?' Mum said, trying to keep calm. The fat of her upper arms jiggled and I thought how the needle-mark on her arm looked like a third eye. Gina thumbed her hair behind her ears. She has big ears, which is a good reason for wearing long hair. Karen's ears aren't so big, so her hair is tight. She likes to wear earrings and sometimes a stud in her nose.

'Magee' Gina breathed.

You'd know Gina was lying. But you'd have to know her to know. A signpost doesn't come up on her head to tell you. Her soul has little ingredients: a drop of blush on her cheeks, a line of worry down her forehead, the way her forefinger touches the corner of her lip. Mum knows how to read the signs too. But she lets on she doesn't. I think it's because she can read other signs I haven't learned to read yet.

Then Adam slunk away, shoulders hunched. He used to suffer from asthma, and kept an inhaler in his pocket. We could count on him going into hospital for a week every year, mostly when the fog rolled down from the mountain, or in summer when the sun was blistering. But he sort of grew out of it during a time when everyone thought he'd have asthma forever. Dad used to look at Adam like a sun-worshipper looking at a grey day, with disappointment. Victor said Dad failed to realise that Adam cared nothing for him either – each was bad weather to the other.

Karen shook her head. She's not really into fellas, she says. She's never going to get married or have babies. Ever. She used to like playing with my Action Men. Victor said it was because Action Man had no penis, and therefore did not constitute a threat to her.

Mum said to Karen, 'Do you know who this fucker is?'

'No,' gulped Karen, 'I don't.'

She sat on her knees on the chair, elbows on the table, hands supporting her chin, looking at Gina as though she were watching a TV soap.

'Where did you meet this lad?' Mum said.

'At a disco … Nijinski's.'

'When?'

'About two months ago.'

'Where does he live?'

Gina froze, then she broke down; tears streamed down her cheeks. Her shuddering something terrible.

Her hands slapping her face, and when that didn't hurt her enough, they started tugging at her lovely red hair. Mum and Karen pulling at her, trying to get her to stop, which I thought was all weird, given that Gina was doing to herself what Mum wanted to do to her. They stopped her just as Victor touched my arm and nodded for us to leave. That's something I like about Victor. He knows when it's the right time to leave. He doesn't wait to be told, like I normally do. In our bedroom, he climbed onto the top bunk. The springs squeaked like crazy. The bunks were bought from a neighbour's Going Away to a Madhouse Clearance Sale. Mrs Travis lived about a mile away in a sorry-looking cottage. Victor says she has these sales every time the world gets her down, which is becoming a fairly frequent occurrence with her.

She's a tall, stiff-backed woman, with steel-wool grey hair and a glass eye. No one knows how she lost the eye. Dad said some kid hit her in the eye with a stone. But I think he said that to stop us throwing stones at each other during our war games. And we did. Last thing I wanted was to meet Mrs Travis with an eye like hers. Victor said we'd be like eejits looking at each other, not wanting to look at each other. Sometimes I have nightmares about Mrs Travis taking her eye out in front of me and asking if we could swap.

Victor sighed. And I couldn't see him do it but I was sure he picked his nose. His voice sounded muffled. Sometimes it bugs me just to know people are doing something even though I can't see or hear them. I told him to quit.

'I only do it when I'm thinking hard.'

'Yeah, what are you thinking hard about now?' I knew it wasn't *Robinson Crusoe* or Mrs Travis.

'There's no such person as Terry Magee.'

'How do you know that, Victor?'

'I just do. It doesn't take a genius.'

Then he said he was going asleep, which meant he wasn't but that he didn't want me disturbing him. When Victor doesn't want to talk, it means there's something really serious on his mind.

I couldn't sleep. In the middle of the night I heard Karen shushing Gina to quieten her tears, telling her everything would be okay. Mum wasn't up. Those nights she was sleeping in the utility room. She told us that Dad's snoring drove her crazy. He didn't seem to mind her absence too much, and Mum didn't harp on about his visits to Dublin, where he stayed in a hotel to meet his rugby friends. Victor says Adam told him that Dad hung his dirty linen on someone else's clothesline. Victor said he'd never seen Dad watch a rugby match on TV, or go to see one being played. He wouldn't even watch Ireland playing on the telly, not even if they were winning. Victor says Mum and Dad had reached an agreement of sorts: to spend as little time as possible in each other's company. He says that's why Father Toner and Kay Walsh call round a lot, to help Mum, and to give her some decent company for a change, outside of us, that is.

Father Pat wears thick glasses that make his grey eyes look all wild and crazy. And his fair hair is lank and greasy-looking. We called him 'Six Six Six'. I didn't know why until Victor told me, and then I stopped calling him it. Father Pat isn't a devil – it's too creepy to even think of.

In the morning, Adam wouldn't get out of bed when Dad called him. He kept the key turned in the lock and said nothing. Dad said three sheep were slaughtered by dogs in the fox covert and he needed Adam's help to cart them away. He wouldn't look for us, because Mum said that Saturday mornings were a study period for us, Easter Holidays and all other holidays included. Adam wasn't so bright in school. Mum used to send him to Mrs Travis for grinds, and while he improved, he still didn't get good enough grades. Mum said she wanted us to get into the habit of working hard. She said Adam just wouldn't work and blamed his asthma for setting him back. Victor said she wanted to keep us away from Dad.

Mum sat at the bay window, staring at the apple blossoms blowing across the yard like pink snowflakes. I wondered if she was mad at me for not picking up the lawn shavings. Victor had said to leave the grass. It had begun to rain. I don't mind the rain so much, but Victor said I should, because rain wears people down, makes them old and bent over before their time. I think it was just an excuse to quit early.

Victor's a little lazy, I've noticed. But twins are twins, and we stick together, and I listen to him, because he wasn't born first for nothing. Mum sipped at her tea. We don't like her silence. Gina and Karen came in with faces full of hope, praying that no one would notice them. Mum didn't stop looking through the window when she said, 'Who is he?'

Gina didn't answer. Mum made a go for her. Gina's not the smartest, but she's smart enough to keep the length of the kitchen table from Mum. I haven't seen Mum so mad since she found a hotel bill in Dad's pocket. She went looper and around then she moved into the utility room. Dad hit Mum once during those awful weeks and under her eye was marked for a long time. Mum's brothers appeared on the doorstep one morning and collared Dad, leading him away somewhere. When he came back he was hardly able to walk. His lips were cut and his nose was a mess. I like Uncle Frank. He's funny. Uncle Tom's a dryshite, Victor says. He never smiles, or passes small talk. I don't like to hear Victor bad-mouth Tom – we have the same sort of noses. Frank's a soldier, and Tom trains racehorses. He told Dad he'd train his horses for him but Dad said no.

'Who!' Mum screamed.

Victor nudged me, but I couldn't bring myself to move.

'Tell me!' Mum said, a step off a scream, hands shovelling her brown hair.

Karen whispered, 'I know.'

Silence, as Mum glared at Karen, her eyes like a vice grip. It seemed to me that Mum knew who the father was, but just needed to hear the name said out loud.

'Go on, say it.'

Her shoulders were raised. She looked like someone bracing herself before a crash.

Karen let the name out with a cry and half-screech. Victor paled. My insides felt sick.

'No, no … no,' Mum said, as if every bit of wind behind her sails had died.

Dad!

Victor started trembling. The three women started to cry and hug each other and all that. Victor and me, we felt as though we were somehow guilty of something. Later, Victor told me that men doing what Dad did gave decent mickies like us a hard time. That when women get mad with a bad man they lump us all together.

Adam rushed in. He had been drinking. You could see it in his eyes. He smoked hash too, or so Victor said. He supposed Adam had to do something in life to take his mind off following in Dad's sheepshit-stained wellies. There was a flicker of hope in his eyes, as though someone he hated had died and he could outwardly grieve but inwardly smile.

'What's happening?' he said, cautiously.

No one wanted to tell him.

'It's that bollocks, isn't it?' he said.

His eyes bored into Gina, hot and hard. Gina nodded weakly, almost reluctantly. Then he said he was going to get the shotgun and blow the bastard's head off. Gina smiled between sobs and said there were no cartridges. We broke out laughing, the lot of us. If anyone looked in the room and saw us all laughing they'd say we should be locked up with Mrs Travis.

Perhaps if there'd been cartridges and Gina had shot Dad, and killed him, then all the stuff that happened mightn't have happened.

We quietened when we saw Dad's jeep fill some of the kitchen window. He's short and heavy. His shoulders are rounded and he has a bit of a rise on his back. Victor called him 'Quasi,' after Quasimodo, but no one cracked up like before.

When he came in he took off his cap and touched the side of the teapot. Noticing the silence, he said, 'Bloody dogs worrying the sheep.'

'You bastard!' Mum said, her eyes scalding.

'What…' he said, his features turning stone-coloured. He took in Adam. His tongue fell from his mouth; no room for it there any longer.

Mum lunged at him. Dad pushed her away, knocking her to the floor. A shocked look at her own lightness registered on Mum's face. Victor tugged at my elbow and left without me. He said he'd studied Adam. How the vein in his neck throbbed, how grey with rage he'd become. Attacking Dad, he ended up holding his jaw, the girls rushing to stand between them.

I went to Mum and helped her to her feet. Karen touched Adam's cheek and Gina said nothing, just rubbed her hands on her jeans as she backed to the window, her eyes on Dad and Adam before flicking to Mum.

Dad raised a finger and went to say something. His eyes watery, his whole frame panting and wheezing. But Mum screamed at him to leave and then plucked her mobile from her handbag and hit the digits.

'The guards … you get out of here, you dirty, filthy bastard.'

Dad turned, kicked at the door and stormed out. We didn't expect to see him again.

He emptied the bank account and flogged the sheep and the Land Rover. The horses he left, which didn't say much for them, in spite of Uncle Tom's optimism. Adam went missing the next day. Victor said he snapped. He worried us out of our minds – except Gina, that is, who didn't seem to care about anything any more. Me? I've been sick from the moment Adam ran away. Secrets make you sick if you leave them too long inside you. I think I'll always be a little sick.

2

Milly

This wasn't how things were meant to turn out. Too much of a dreamer, that's my problem. Look where it got me. Thinking of *him* as the perfect husband, the one with the halo over his mickey. The dirty *bastard*. God, I need a cigarette. Mike, you bastard! Why? Was I not enough for you? Your own daughter, your own son. Christ, how could you? What sort of a fucking animal are you?

The baby's crying. Gina's. A scrunched-up little thing with powerful lungs. He hasn't stopped crying since we brought him home. Babies sense things. An atmosphere in a house is picked up by a baby the same way we pick up a smell of fresh paint. No one has mentioned a name for him. If Gina or Karen suggest 'Adam' I'll scream the walls down. Honest to fuck, I will. My nerves are all over the place. I think the kids see the way I am and try to leave me alone as much as possible. There are times I have to shout

16

at them to get the space I need. Jesus, how I fight for that space.

When Father Pat told me about Adam I went numb all over. I think I smiled. This was a mistake. Surely. My Adam wouldn't do such a thing. Not him. To himself.

Not true. I think I farted. I'm sure I did. I always do when my nerves come at me. I remember doing my exams and I couldn't handle the Maths, and I started to panic and I just couldn't stop doing it. I really couldn't. Julie used to say it was hereditary, that an aunt of ours had the same problem. There's medicine you can take. I'm taking it at the moment. It's doing the trick.

I met Pat through Kay. He's a pleasant sort, conscious of his weight. He's very heavy, and he smokes these thin cigars his brother sends him from America. I like his laugh, the way small things amuse him so much, the way he takes them to heart. If he takes the nasty side of life to heart then he must have huge problems. I think when he's up he's in the clouds and when he's down he loses sight of himself. He gets depressed but says he's coping. Prozac helps. It helps a lot. Viagra for the mind, he calls it.

He stood there in the porch, the rain teeming behind him, his grey eyes large behind his glasses, full of tears, his fingers mingling with each other. I had hoped he was going to tell me that Mike was dead. I would put on a sad face, perhaps even read a poem in church. Play the dutiful widow. But life doesn't parcel up problems for you to post and be shut of. I didn't expect his thin lips to breathe *Adam*. Why should my son die? There was no need for him to die. He had his whole life in front of him. It's unnatural to give birth to a son and then see the life gone from him, the open ground swallow him. It did something to me. Turned something, gave me a dark spot in my heart.

My son is six months dead today. It is early morning. The hands on the cuckoo clock are fastened at quarter to six, a cuckoo clock which hasn't worked for ages. Adam's fingers the last to hold it, the last to try and repair it; but in the end he had to smile defeat – the pieces lying about on the table were ones he said were extra and not needed by the clock to function.

He said it mystified him why the second hand refused to tick. He understood why I valued the clock. Julie gave it to me for my fortieth birthday. Stuffing all the pieces back, he shrugged. Cause of death unknown, he said, which is more that I can say about his. Cause of death, known, the reasons not as clear-cut, but a little clearer to me than it is to others.

For my fortieth birthday, Julie drove me to Newbridge and parked in the Mall there, not far from the Woodcraft factory in which I used to work, where I met Mike, who came in with an invoice. It was a scorching day and I wore no bra. We liked each other from the word 'go'. Sometimes I wonder if there's something wrong with me – how could I end up loving a man like Mike? Have five children with him? Two after I found I no longer loved him. I mean, how did I let that happen? What sort of fool am I? If I'd gotten rid of him years ago, then Adam might still be alive, Gina might not have had a child and my other kids wouldn't be looking at me as though I'd gone mad. If I had done that – got rid of him – things would have turned out differently.

Mike! Tall, handsome Mike with the firm belly, who became Mike with the paunch, and then Mike with the beer belly. I suppose he graduated like that in sexual tastes too. It sickens me to think about it, so I don't; I mean I try not to think about his hands on me, my kids. Touching me, touching … touching … *them*.

In Newbridge that day, Julie, who was younger than me by about two years, said she was going to Cyprus on holiday. Did I want to come? Her treat? That's the sort Julie was. Generous. She worked for a solicitor's firm on the Main Street and had invested wisely what money was left her by Dad. I helped Mike to squander mine. She'd been to Cyprus the year before, and had met a German fella called Daniel Elser.

She stayed in Limassol, in a self-catering apartment with two girls from work: one butch, the other a bitch. The rows between them drove her into having an affair with a not-so-sexy-looking creature; all nose and chin and little under the trouser belt, she giggled, wriggling her little finger. But guess what? He said his grandad was interned in the Curragh Camp during the Second World War. He was a pilot who crash-landed his plane in a field in Wexford and was frog-marched to the local police barracks by pitchfork-wielding locals. Daniel's a nice guy. He came over for Julie's funeral. I think he was keen on her, and he didn't look half as bad as she made him out. Julie had high standards in everything. It's a pity that part of her didn't rub off on me.

I couldn't go to Limassol. Well, you can't up and leave five children. Not with a husband like Mike, who didn't help in the house, who forgot his children had mouths and needed to eat. Who thought a washing machine was a one-channel TV station, watched only by women. Even when they were babies he didn't help out. There were evenings I was knackered and fit for nothing only a long sleep, and the kids would either be sick, or in need of a feed, or both, and he wouldn't lift a finger. That's the way he was, and that's the way I let him be. I was a right fool.

We'd a great day. In spite of the rain. After a Chinese meal Julie brought me to The Square, where we took in a picture, eating popcorn like we were kids all over. The movie wasn't great, but if I ever see it again, on TV like you always do after a couple of years, I'll think of Julie, the popcorn bucket on her lap, and her telling me that Harrison Ford was her ideal man. If there's such a thing as an ideal man.

It's dark outside. So dark. Dark as my husband's soul. Adam's suicide letter is on the coffee table, by my mug of cold coffee, beside an ashtray full of ash and cigarette ends. The things he says make me wonder if I lived in the same house as him; had all what he'd written taken place under my roof? Four pages. Written in red biro. Why couldn't I reach him, why couldn't he reach me? Jesus, I was here for him, am here for the others. Why? Why did he reject me? Why wasn't I an option for him?

I feel sorry for Adam. I miss him. I am angry with him. There are times I can't believe that Adam, who I cradled in my arms the moment he was born, is gone. My son has come and is no more, leaving me words as a means of explanation. Words about Mike. Words about himself, his feelings, how he felt good in himself for doing what he was going to do. A self-punishment.

His hands. I remember his baby fingers gripping my small finger, the sit of him on my lap, the softness of his head resting against my breasts, and through the years all the affection he gave, his telling me he loved me, all changing when he reached seven or eight, and the baby ways left him, or what I thought at the time were the baby ways leaving him, instead of realising that the world was taking him.

Taking the letter, I fold and envelope it. It's important that no one else reads Adam's writings. For my eyes only. Though Gina certainly wouldn't want to read its contents, or Karen for that matter. They have a natural fear of how much it would take out of them. But Victor and Morris are a different story. Twins. Unidentical in looks and character. Victor is bright and handsome, with Mike's dark looks and droll sense of humour. It is he who worries me. He spends a lot of time in Adam's room. I find it strange that he should have been closer to an older brother than his twin. While Victor looks at you in a way that I sometimes find bothersome, Morris looks at you differently, as if he were taking on some of your hurting. Victor's eyes blame. Accuse. Smoulder.

It's raining hard. Awful rain. I think of Adam lying in his grave outside Newbridge.

They're building new houses in the next field. The workers kept busy during the funeral service; hammering, and shouting at each other. No mark of respect shown for a young boy, a young life. It felt like no one cared.

You can smell the Curragh air from there, fresh and scented with furze. You can see red sunsets, the skies caped with beautiful colours, and on early mornings and late evenings, you can breathe in the peace. A peace and tranquillity that'd make you envious of the dead.

Julie. On the phone. Saturday. Washing machine on its last tumble. One more load, then that's it. There was a water shortage and we had a reduced supply on uneven dates. I wanted to get finished. I could have done without Julie's call, as much as Julie could have done without her news.

Sobs.

'What's wrong – Julie, tell me?'

'Come over, will you, please, Milly.'

Putting the phone down, I sighed. Sometimes Julie was like Mum. She'd get down in herself for days. Julie had Mum's deep-blue eyes and Dad's fair hair. She had a figure that was, even after she'd dieted, still lumpy. She envied me my figure and wanted to know how I did it – with five kids. I said they're the reason. When you're pregnant the baby pulls you out of shape, and when you're running around after them, doing this and that, you go back into shape. Granted, with a few stretch-marks. Badges of Honour. I didn't suspect then that Julie had a serious problem, so on the way over I was giving out about her to myself.

Julie let me in, eased the door shut behind me. She sniffled.

'Julie?'

'I've got cancer.'

'No, oh God.'

She nodded, took my hand. Little sisters again. Each nudging the other into seeing where the spider was in our bedroom. She didn't have to tell me where she had it.

'Like Mum?' I said.

A small nod. Threads of her fair hair fastened to her cheeks with tears. Breast cancer. Losing one, then the other. Delaying death. Slowing it up, but not enough in Mum's case, nor, as it turned out, in Julie's. I stayed with her that night, and lots of other nights, was with her when she died in a hospital ward on a cold February night. She died hard. She didn't die fighting, she died wanting to die, but her illness played games with her.

I asked Father Pat about it, about Christ and his religion. To be fair to him, he just shook his head and said nothing. I don't know how a priest prays. I really fucking don't.

He didn't say anything, which was good, because nothing was what I wanted to hear from him. He just gave me his arms. I shouldn't say 'just' because it meant more to me than that. A lot more.

Pat's an orphan. You talk about things with someone who's suffered as much if not more than you have. Well, I could, and I did. When he was five years old his parents went off the road in Galway. His grandparents brought him up, he said, his lift of lips suggesting it was a task performed from a sense of duty rather than one of love.

Cleaning out Julie's flat afterwards, I burned all her travel brochures. And was trying to deal with her death when Gina hit me with her news. Then Adam did what he did. Now, I'm trying to deal with Julie's and Adam's deaths. I'm trying to sort out my feelings for a baby who isn't mine. Who resembles a man I hate. I'm worried about Karen, Victor and Morris. Wonder if they were abused. Shaking like a wind-blown leaf inside, because if they were, I don't know what I'll do. I don't think I can take much more. I'm trying to think straight, but my thoughts are all over the place, and I feel sick inside. Always sick inside. If it weren't for Kay and Father Pat, I don't think I could cope, if what I am doing can be called coping.

They say I mustn't blame myself, and yet who else is at fault? It's me. It's not as if I didn't have my suspicions about Mike, I did, but I buried them, telling myself that he was bad, but not that bad. Saying to myself that if he touched the kids they'd tell me. Well, they didn't.

I thought I'd done everything to keep Mike in check. When I found out he was visiting a brothel in Dublin, I didn't walk out. I didn't send for Frank or Tom, my younger brothers, to sort him out. I just bit my tongue and went into the utility room, telling the kids that Dad's snoring was keeping me awake. Of course, it's easy not to care what your husband does with another woman when you don't care for him.

Frank and Tom sorted Mike out before. I'm closest to Frank. He has thinning fair hair and carries a scar above his left eyebrow. He reminds me of a dog he used to own. A Kerry Blue that lived for fighting and getting into all sorts of roguery. Mike's terrified of Frank. He acts as if he isn't, but he is. His eyes used do his running away for him. Frank thumped Mike for hitting me. Came in and told me that if that fucker ever thought of laying a finger on me again, I was to call him. I felt guilty, and a little angry at him for hurting Mike. I guess I'm odd in some ways. Julie, who told Frank about my eye, said I should be grateful to Frank. Look at all the women in the country who'd like to have a brother to stand up for them.

We grew up in terraced quarters on the Curragh Camp. Dad was a soldier, a corporal in the military police. At night we'd lie in bed and listen to his Land Rover passing the house and fall asleep with a feeling of being safe. Then, when he left the army, we moved to Newbridge. I missed the Curragh, how I'd wake in the mornings and look out the window, and see the gold on the furze, the Wicklow mountains, sometimes catch the soldiers on exercise, or see them running in block by the house, singing songs like, '*I know a biddy with a rubber diddy ....*'

It seems cruel now. But back then, before Mum got the illness, it was a joke song at breakfast, when we'd laugh about it, and wonder how Frank was getting on in his platoon. We ate army eggs with government stamps on their shells, and used army toilet paper that was hard on your arse and which Julie blamed for her piles. Kay and me used to go to the pictures – we paired off once with Zambian cadets we met outside a timber-framed shop. Kay was a bitch. She filled the balcony with loud laughter till Old Dillon, the usher, gave them their marching orders, walking them out under a flood of torchlight. Afterwards she told me she couldn't stop laughing – each time he went to kiss her, his lips almost swallowed her.

'You're racist, Kay Walsh.'

'I am not. He's a lovely fella, but honest to God, I'm telling you the truth, I felt like a toilet bowl after a plunger had got at it.'

We screamed laughter. The two of us, walking home. Kay's fella broke it off with her afterwards, said she hadn't kissable lips. I wonder where those chaps ended up. If they're alive. God, I'm only forty-two and the Curragh seems so long ago. Another lifetime. Look at me. I didn't think I'd end like this, a skinny, cigarette-puffing mother of five. Narrow face wrinkled up. My hair thin, its youthful shine long gone. I'd always been happy with my hair, its shine, its texture. Long brown hair.

I wonder what Julie'd make of all this. What Mum and Dad would think. They'd be hurt, and feel sorry for me and my family. Frank's in Lebanon. He's returning soon. He came home for Adam's funeral and has written to tell Gina that he'd stand for the child. Tom takes care of the horses. He keeps telling me one is promising. He wants to bring them over to his yard. It'd be easier for him, I know, stop him running back and forth so much, but honest to God I can't think straight enough to give an answer to anything.

My eldest child is dead. He should not be dead. There are times I feel so fucking angry with him that I can't bring myself to pray for him. He's buried close to Julie. I haven't been able to go visit his grave yet. I don't know where I'm going or what I'm doing. And although Father Pat and Kay are kind, and offer suggestions, I feel as though I've come to the end of the road. I miss Adam. God, how I miss him. I can't take to the baby. If he looked like Gina I think I would, sooner or later.

There's a gentle cough behind me. I get a start.

Gina looks at me. Her hair is tossed and she's been crying. I think she cried her baby to sleep.

'How long have you been there?' I ask, pocketing Adam's letter, blinking away a tear I didn't know had formed.

'I'm making some hot chocolate – you want some, Mum?'

'No. He's gone off?'

'Yes. I hope he sleeps, I'm exhausted.'

'He should – you should try and get some sleep yourself.'

She's wearing that long pink gown Julie bought her for her last birthday. I think all the kids are missing their sugar-aunt.

'I can't.' She sits on the edge of the sofa, looks at the bunny tails on her slippers. So much of her still a child, so little of her a real mother. She'd suffered having the baby. Forceps and stitches. I went into the labour ward with her. Prayers running on dual tracks;

one for Gina, and one for Mike: that his balls meet with a razor.

'What am I going to do, Mum?' she says, not crying. She knows I couldn't handle it.

'Put him up for adoption and get on with your life.'

'It's not his fault. Not Eric's fault he's here. Why should he suffer? Who's going to want me if they find out who's the father? They'll get rid of me too. Won't they?'

Her thoughts are like mine, scattered.

She's named him. Eric. Good. At least she didn't call him Adam. I couldn't live with his name being aired all about the place. I want to put Adam, Julie and Mike into small boxes in my mind. I've got to do it, because the others need me, and in my mind's eye, the spectre of Adam's tree looms above the lot of them. If one child can commit suicide (I hate that word), then so can the others – *five green bottles*.

'What happened wasn't your fault, Gina.'

'Why do you make me feel as if it is?'

Do I? Perhaps so. Moving toward her, she shifts a little on the sofa, as though she were frightened of me. I put my arm round her and she rests her head against my breasts. And sobs. I cry too. But my tears come softly. I've got to be strong, for them. For me. Plans? Leave here, that's one. Leave Kildare, Newbridge, leave every sodding place that reminds me of the hurts, leave every sodding face whose eyes tell me they know about me, my family. Have read the papers, and know. Their eyes asking what I ask myself. How did a mother living at home not know about these things? How? Is she stupid? Blind? How in God's name could she not have known?

Well, I didn't. I didn't. I didn't. I didn't. Did not know.

An ordinary mother, bringing up an ordinary family, that's all I ever wanted to be. Mike and Adam have knocked the ordinariness out of us. Gina's mind is in an uproar. Therapy might help, but the truth of what happened is going to grow up alongside her. Staring her square in the face, every day.

So many thoughts drumming in my head.

Julie's Box: her lying in a hospital bed, staring through a window frame that had become her picture of life. A prisoner in her own body. Her passing a release for both of us, but less so for me.

Adam's Box: a boy in a cowboy suit with a bright-red sheriff's star, and capgun sounding, on Christmas morning. Chubby and cheerful, growing thin and moody. All the times I asked myself why he turned so morose, so rebellious, when I should have been asking him. Now I can read all about it, whenever I want, by scanning down red-biroed lines that I suspect he meant to pass as being written in blood.

Gina's Box: the lid is half-closed. She's looking out, and I'm looking in. Neither of us knowing what to do about what we see.

These are things I tell Kay when she comes over the next morning. Kay's heavyset and single. The Merry

Spinster she calls herself. She still works in the old factory, screwing the manager when his wife is away. She's hilarious. She says he used to keep promising her he'd leave his wife when the kids were grown.

Now they've grown, he keeps talking about his grandkiddies. It hasn't sunk in with him that Kay prefers the arrangement. That she's using him, and not the other way round.

In the sitting-room she smiles, and says, 'A bad night?'

'Yeah, Kay.'

She studies the eye of her cigarette and tames a cough with the back of her hand. She has a habit of touching the bridge of her glasses to shift them further up her nose. She has a fat, lovely face, full of kindness. I don't think we ever had a falling out, except that time she went into the Kissogram business and wanted me to be her partner. The things that one did. Honestly. She's Adam's godmother, and sometimes she cries with me, but more often than not she lends me her shoulder.

'Have you heard from....'

'No.'

Mike didn't come home for the funeral. I think he might have called a couple of times, but he hung up when I answered.

Kay shakes her head, pinches her earring. She says Father Pat said he'll be over this afternoon. He's trying to persuade me to have the whole family receive counselling. I know he's trying to be good,

31

and maybe I will as soon as I can think straight. Right now, I can't.

God, I feel sick, all over. My body aches, my mind aches. Kay says the worst is over but I feel it isn't. In fact, I'm frightened that the worst hasn't happened yet.

3

Morris

August

The baby still looks like Dad. He bawls morning, noon and night. Victor says with all the whinging he does it's like having Dad back in the house again. But at least Mum and Gina are on friendly terms, speaking with each other, and no tension in their tones, no words poised to hiss and hurt. It's like there's a weight lifted from the shoulders of the house. A small weight.

Karen's pissed off a little with Gina for calling the baby Eric. She wanted to call him Leonardo, after the guy who sank to death in the *Titanic*, after he froze. I didn't like the film. If I were that guy I'd have let the girl throw herself into the sea. She was very beautiful, but I didn't like the way she turned out, all old and wrinkled up, and as I far as I'm concerned, if she really loved that fella she wouldn't have married another lad and had babies for him, she'd have joined a convent or something. But then, that's me. Karen thinks that I have a bad way of looking at things. Life doesn't stop because someone's dead, she said. I don't think she'd say that now, not with Adam gone, not off the top of her head, anyway.

I used to like watching war films and all, but now if I see someone getting killed on the screen I sort of shudder inside. I can't help thinking that the poor fellow who got shot is someone's Dad or Son or *Brother*. I know it's acting and that, and the blood isn't real. It's Adam, I think. Six months ago today he hung himself.

Victor's lying on his bunk, reading *Robinson Crusoe*. Mum bought him *Swiss Family Robinson* but he hasn't got round to reading it yet. One of these days, Victor's going to head off and find his little island in the sun. I like reading horror stories. I always read the first two and the last two pages – if anything happens to the hero at the end I don't read the book. I like happy endings. My English teacher says it's a good way to be, to know what I want from a story. The important thing is to read, he says.

I'm lying on the bottom bunk. Dressed, but most of me not wanting to start the day.

'Victor?'

He doesn't answer, which doesn't mean he didn't hear. Although he could have his headphones on. Sometimes shuts me out. Sometimes I think I only put up with him because he knows so much, and tells me a lot. When he told me about Crusoe having a Man Friday, and maybe being queer, I had to ask what he meant. I didn't like what he had to say, and I didn't think he was funny when he said we could turn out as a pair of queers too. He said our hormones were making their minds up. I don't think I'd like to be queer. Victor says I have no choice. I hope I'm not queer.

I asked him how would I know if I were a gay man. He said, 'homosexuals', drawing the word out, 'like boys better than girls'. He said I was to look at a picture of a boy's naked butt and then a girl's, and whichever one excites me most and makes Neddy go hard, then I'll know if I'm gay or not.

Easy peasy. I asked him what I would be if I found both pictures exciting. He took a deep, deep breath, and said I'd be some fella to watch out for, a hundred per cent pervert. He said I should take a look at Karen's arse sometime. I said I wouldn't expect to feel the same way for my sister's arse as I would for anyone else's. He went quiet and then grunted something I couldn't make out, and then fell quiet again. A disturbed peace hung in the air. I asked had he any pictures of naked women but he didn't answer. I got thick with him for ignoring me.

Neddy – that's what we call our mickies. Dad's younger brother, Neddy, came home a few weeks before Adam died. Dad says he's a proper flute. I was out back playing with the rusty tractor behind the stables, in a place where nettles and thistles were knee-high, and which I'd beaten down with a stick that was a sword in my hand slaying snakes and not stinging plants. There's rats, too, big ones. I asked Mum for a dog a long time ago. A dog would kill rats. This place would be Heaven to him. I don't like cats. I love dogs.

Dad and Neddy were arguing. Neddy wanted Dad to give him a site to build a house and some money. If he did that, he'd forget all about what Dad did to him years ago. They were at the side of the stables. They didn't see me. Dad told him to fuck off and not to come around again. A free site and some money. Dad gave nothing away of himself, not unless there was something in it for him. Neddy has a squeaky voice and what he was saying was drowned out by Dad's angry words. I never saw Neddy after that; none of us did. I was called for dinner and had to sneak the long way round, by the length of the stables and behind the long shed, so as to avoid Dad and Neddy.

I was having a great time on the tractor too, pretending I was a master mechanic trying to breathe life into an engine that hadn't ticked over for twenty years. These days I seem to be pretending a lot.

'Victor!'

'What do you want?'

'We have to go feed the horses.'

'You go.'

'No – that's not fair.'

'You like horses, don't you? You do it. Stop bothering me.'

'Frank and Tom said we were both to do it. Right?'

Springs squeaking, he throws his feet to the floor. Lately, I think we're crowding in on each other. Sometimes I think he's edging me into fighting with him. He has taken down my Man United poster from the ceiling and put up Arsenal's.

He doesn't even follow the Gunners, he likes West Ham, but he won't stick a picture up of them, they're so useless. We used to keep the room tidy but he doesn't do his share any more. The way he keeps going into Adam's room I think he has his eyes set on moving in there.

'Come on, then, moany hole,' Victor says.

Gina's in the kitchen, feeding the brat. Mum's sipping coffee and smoking, staring as usual through the bay window, probably taking in the privet hedge I cut crooked, or the leaves that were beginning to fall from the apple blossoms. Swimming in her thoughts again – sometimes she drives me mad. I've enough to worry about without worrying about her too. Can't she see the change in Victor?

Karen's reading a Mills and Boon. Her small nose gives little twitches. There's a smell of shitty Pampers in the air and baby powder. Women are hard to make out. They all want Eric at different times and don't want him at other times. Mum is doing her share with him, but there's no love in it for her. She might as well be feeding the horses. Gina's half mad. Baby blues, Victor says. She shouts and screams a lot. Karen grabs the baby when she gets in a mood. That little fellow doesn't know how lucky he is to be alive. Of the three women in our house, Karen's the only one who'd shed a tear for him if he died. Mum, I think, has hardened her heart. A couple of times Gina's after being caught shaking the shite out of Eric; only for Karen we'd have a murdered baby on our hands.

'Put some toast on for your breakfast, lads,' Mum says. She doesn't look at us. I can almost see the scratch marks on her temples where she tears at her nerves.

Victor says, 'Yeah, right,' and gives me a middle finger.

There are some people who think feeding themselves is more important than feeding others. I shoot him with a pair of fingers and go out back.

From the rear of our house you can see Kildare's round tower. I climbed it once. It smelled of old stone and old timber. From the top you can see all around for miles and miles: loads of different greens, and everyone going about their business, a train pulling from the station, a football game in the park, the ball lofted high between the posts, making my feet itch to kiss the ball. I imagined the Vikings down below, and boiling oil or water falling on them, their screams, and the monks saying '*Fuck them, fuck ye*'.

Things were rough in those days: no electricity, no radio or TV. The Dark Ages is right, but some of the goings of that time are still going on, and on.

The horses are ninnying as I make my way to the barn. Slowcoaches. And old. I think one of them might have won a race a long time ago. Dad said the grey one did in England. But you couldn't trust his tongue, as we've all found out.

Like me, the horses turn their heads when Frank arrives in his red jeep and cuts the engine right beside me. His door has small dents and the windscreen is cracked. When he gets drunk he crashes the jeep. Mum and Tom are always giving out to him, and he just grimaces and says, 'Yeah, I shouldn't be driving with drink on me.'

'Morning, Morris,' he says, closing the door.

He's wearing a grey Adidas tracksuit top and jeans. His loafers have specks of blood on them, which tells me he shaved with them on. He has a bit of toilet paper stuck under his chin. His thin lips sometimes make you think they disappear inside, kissing some hurting going on in his heart.

'Where's Victor?'

'Stuffing his face.'

Frank smiles, glides a hand over his hair, 'I'll be taking them away today – there's a box coming.'

'Where to?'

'Tom's – he's going to try and get the grey ready for a race.'

I put Frank under scrutiny. He's lightly tanned from being in the Lebanon. He's an infantry sergeant who gets to fire rifles and machine guns, sometime rockets. He's been to Iraq, Cyprus, Bosnia, and Lebanon. He was married once but it broke up. I don't know how. I think Detta was too pretty to be left alone for long periods. She's a model, with high cheekbones and blond hair. Mum said she wasn't made for the rough road and Frank was a rough road. They've a son, but him and his mum are in America, living near Disneyland. Now and then Mum gets postcards of Mickey Mouse and Goofy from Detta. She says Detta's just trying to make us jealous. Victor says we're easy to make jealous. We would be jealous of Detta if she sent us a card from Hell. Frank goes over to visit every year. He always brings us back presents, usually T-shirts with famous wrestlers' faces on them. He stops drinking for about a month before flying out there. He wants to fool Detta into thinking he's getting along fine without her.

I hope Frank's not telling me lies about the horses, and that Tom is taking them in. I find it hard to trust anyone these days.

Adam liked the grey. He wouldn't like to know he was leaving. Then if he thought that much of him, he shouldn't have hung himself. He should have stayed and looked after the horse. Fancy Lad and Bright Star, Dad called them. To Adam they were Hulk Hogan and The Dragon – Adam loved watching the wrestling. He'd stay up late at night to watch them. Once, Dad got Sky Sports turned off so Adam couldn't watch his heroes in action. Mum went ballistic when she heard and had it turned back on, and then she bought Adam two wrestling tapes. The way Dad looked at Adam is a way I hope I never catch myself looking at anyone, never mind my son.

Frank claps his hands. You'd think it was cold out or something. It is a clear day, still and quiet, the way days are when a fog lifts. He says he has something to ask me. Then I realised an idea had escaped him, and he'd clapped hands to capture it, like I used to do with bubbles Victor blew. I'd catch some of the bubbles on my forefinger, and take in the oil colours in them, the colour of a spill of petrol on a road, and when I burst them they smelled of suds.

'Yeah, Frank?'

'Do you want to come camping with me – yourself and Victor?'

Camping? I felt a little afraid at first, but then Uncle Frank isn't Dad. But then I didn't know that Dad was like Dad until....

'I don't know, Frank.'

'Come on … it'll be a break and good fun.'

'Where?'

'Mayo – Westport. Galway – we'll go fishing, climb a mountain or two. Tom has a horse going in Galway … it'll be worth seeing.'

'Okay then, will you ask Mum?'

We were due back to school Monday week, so Frank must be bringing us away on Monday. Mum'll probably ask him to bring Eric, and leave him somewhere, which'd be funny if she weren't serious.

Frank left, taking Mum's messages list with him. Mum calls me in. I'd been talking with the horses, saying how much I'd miss them, telling them lies, really. I never had much to do with the horses. Dad and Adam took care of them. The horses were just there for me, like the hens, the broken-down tractor all rusted up, the old shed no one ever went into because it had huge cobwebs and Frank said the biggest rats he ever saw. A foot long, and they'd eat their way inside you like that – click-of-fingers quick. Its loosely fitting black doors were locked but you could peep inside, through the crack between them. There's nothing interesting in there. A garage pit covered with thick floorboards, bits of old straw and heaps of hessian sacking. A dank smell and another of stale oil. Separate smells, as if each had chosen a different nostril to climb.

Mum sits in at the table. I thought how the bay window must miss her eyes. Gina sits holding Eric, Victor toys with a salt cellar and Karen drinks her Evian. She's always drinking water, purifying her system she says. She's into being perfect.

'Now,' Mum says, 'there's a counsellor coming to have a chat with us….'

Victor says, 'What?'

Karen says, 'Do we need to?'

Gina sighs, 'Mum … for God's sake.'

'It'll do us no harm,' Mum says, fingers doing a jig on her temples.

'I don't want to see any fucking counsellor,' Victor says, his chin jutting out a little, like a rock breaking sea waters.

Mum breathes in, and then out, 'Okay … okay, but I will, Gina will, and Karen will.'

She turns to me, 'Morris?'

'Yeah, maybe.' First I want to see what Victor has to say before committing myself.

I've got so used to copying Victor that it has become second nature.

Victor says quickly, 'I want to move into Adam's room.'

That hurt me. He made it sound as if I smelled up the room he was in. Mum's pale. She bites her lip to stop her words spilling over.

'We'll see.' Victor nods. He looks my way and says, 'It'll be cool us having our own rooms.'

'Yeah – your very own island.'

He knew I was cutting at him, but said nothing, because he knew he had hurt me. Victor follows me outside. I had to pack the horses' blankets, saddles and stuff into tea chests that Frank left out.

'Why are you mad with me?' he asks, like he doesn't know.

'I'm not mad at you.'

'Thick, then?'

'I'm not thick either.'

'Look, I'm sorry.'

'That's okay.' I say it quickly enough for him to know that it isn't okay. He is placing a barrier between us. A door I'd have to knock on when I wanted to see him. I've never had to knock to get to see him before. He knew I depended on him to fill me in on things. Like the time I went into the bathroom and saw this thing down the toilet. Right off he could tell me what it was.

A period towel, he said. Explaining. Now when the girls are in bad form (all the time lately), we just look at each other and smile when one of us whispers, '*Always*'.

Watching the horses going is sad. A little bit of Adam being horseboxed away. The grey gives a little ninny going through the gate, over the cattle grid. Victor says he is calling us bastards for ditching him. That he'd come back to haunt us as a bar of soap.

But Uncle Frank and Tom aren't like that. Are they? The thing is, after Dad and Adam, we don't know who to believe in any more.

We went for a walk then, up the hill leading to the ruins of a place Dad said was an ancient fort. In summer some people walk up there to have a look around.

You can see the Hill of Allen, and the stand at the Curragh Racecourse. You can see Kildare town too, but you'd have to stand in a bed of thistles. Victor sits on a lichen-covered stone and hawks. The breeze is strong here, so he cups his hands about his cigarette and disposable lighter.

'Want one?'

'No.'

I didn't like to see him smoking. He sometimes came up here with Adam. He said Adam smoked roaches and drank cider. He came here to get away from Dad and from other things.

'Morris,' Victor says.

'Yeah?'

'Tell this counsellor lad nothing, right?'

I run a thumb along my eyebrow.

'Tell him nothing – and blink like hell if he looks into your eye.'

'Why?'

'These counsellors are funny people … you don't want him looking about inside your head … putting things there.'

I was going to say he wouldn't see much there. But he would, I suppose. There's stuff about Adam, about Dad, about Gina, about Mum, about Aunt Julie. About everything really. Maybe he could check things out for me – if I'd a virus or something. Perhaps he could answer questions.

Questions like why did Adam kill himself? Why did Dad give Gina a baby? Why did Aunt Julie die so young? Why did Mrs Travis go mad, and is the tree Adam hung himself from still standing? What's going on in Mum's mind? What did Adam say in his letter? She'd sat us down to have a chat, to tell us about the counsellor, but she'd meant to ask us something else, but hadn't the courage, because she didn't want to find out. Much like she didn't want to find out who was the father of Gina's baby. The question? *Who else did Dad…*.

Victor hauls in the last drags of his cigarette and says, 'Let's go.'

As we make our way down I see Father Toner driving in. He has someone with him. A tall man. Probably just a solicitor to discuss Aunt Julie's will.

There is also the possibility that Dad will use Father Toner as a go-between. A Mister Fix-it. Somehow, I can't imagine Mum letting Dad back in the house. It wouldn't be right. He living under the same roof with his daughters, and his daughter's son by him, it wouldn't look right at all.

Father Toner surfaces from the sitting-room shaking his head. The old man who followed him out says nothing, just leaves his card on the coffee table, then tells Mum that when she feels she is ready, to give him a call, anytime.

Father Toner, when he gets outside, looks at the skies, as if his prayer for us has fallen short. I like him. He gives me the feeling that he always does his best for people and that he'd feel bad in himself if he couldn't help.

Frank asks Mum about bringing us away. She agrees without even thinking about it. I breathe a little easier. Just because she got it wrong about Dad doesn't mean she'll get it wrong about Frank.

Mum goes hyper, getting our clothes out and packing them, saying to herself she must buy us some new gear, especially tracksuits. When she's packed our kitbag, she pauses, goes into Dad's room, telling us to get the firelighters.

All his clothes she piles in a heap outside and then all of Adam's, and every bit of furniture in the two rooms. The clothes don't take off right away, smoking and smelling as though to protest at their burning. It isn't until Victor pours a quart of paraffin over the furniture that the fire takes hold. Adam's mattress is piss-stained. The stain looks like a big yellow eye, closing up when the flames draw inwards.

For a few days Mum and the girls are in great form, but when Victor moves into Adam's room the bad moods return.

4
Victor

Last days of August

They looked at me when I said I wanted to move into Adam's room. Why did it surprise them? It's a big room and it's just going to waste.

After we burned all of Dad's and Adam's things, I moved in that night. Morris wasn't impressed but he gave me a hand to dismantle the bunk bed and haul my half into Adam's bedroom. He said his own bed looked sort of naked without having another one on top. But he admired the ceiling, the logos of a moon, Jupiter, and the stars I'd stuck there. He didn't notice them before, said from his bunk all he saw was my lumpy arse sinking in the bed.

I tried to cheer him up by saying that at least he'd no one farting on top of him any more, but he didn't raise a smile. With his carry-on, anyone would think I was leaving the country instead of just shifting a few feet. I suppose people, when you think about it, are in a different world when they're in their own rooms. *Nobody knows what goes on behind closed doors* are words from a song I heard Dad singing on stage at Uncle Frank's wedding. But Dad, they do know, everyone knows, and what's more, there's more to know, isn't there? You prick.

Watching me remove Adam's nameplate from the door upset Morris a little. It shouldn't have. He's dead and he's not coming back, and the sooner everyone around here realises that the better. I left Morris my Playstation, just to cheer him up, and though it's wonky, a wire loose in the transformer and sometimes the machine just conks out in the middle of a game, he appreciated the gesture.

He loves playing *Donkey Kong*, but gets stuck on the Treehouse level. He's okay, Morris, but not so bright; I mean he doesn't have the sense to know when to quit.

Morris put on a bit of a face when I took the soldier alarm clock. His hangdog expression irked me, so I left him the ceiling poster of the Gunners, knowing he didn't like it and that it would annoy him. I don't know why I like to hurt him. After all, he is my twin, and he's not the smartest kid on the block – needs minding, so the natural inclination should be to take care of him. But I was closer to Adam. He was more of a friend than a brother.

Maybe it's wrong to get too close to people. If you don't get close then it doesn't hurt so much when they die. Your guts won't feel twisted up, and your head doesn't feel as though you've a blow-heater scorching the inside of your skull. Although I think Morris sees things the rest of us don't, but he doesn't realise the significance of what he's seeing.

He saw Mum with Adam's letter. He told me he saw Father Toner giving it to her. He said this to me without thinking about what he was saying, not realising that the letter held the reason why Adam had done away with himself. Perhaps not exact reasons but clues that would fit together in a jigsaw we could see and understand.

It's not important how Adam died. The fact is he's gone and he left without saying anything to me. It hurts. He used to tell me everything. I used to tell him everything. Now I know he had things on his mind that he couldn't tell me, couldn't tell anyone.

I keep expecting Mum to show us the letter, or read it out. Morris says Mum mentioned things to him about it, said that Dad had done things. Morris said she'd been at the Bailey's and was speaking more to herself than anyone else. He'd been out getting a glass of milk and smelled a candle burning. He found the source in the sitting-room, Mum smoking, taking in the eye of the candle – mumbling to herself, as though she were speaking with someone. Morris didn't understand that Mum was praying. He called it acting weird.

Camping. Tomorrow, with Uncle Frank. Four days out of the house, away from the brooding walls, Mum's sad face, Gina's crazy face and Karen's bewildered face. Away from Eric. He doesn't cry so much nowadays. You'd think by him that he believed he had been accepted. If so, he's lulled himself into believing wrongly.

Mum tolerates him because she's afraid not to. Gina loves him but deep down you sense she's asking herself why. And Karen's like a cloud sailing above all the trouble. Unlike clouds, she keeps her dark moments to herself.

This therapist thing bugs me. How can talking about things fix things? All the talking in the world isn't going to bring back my brother. It's all bullshit really. You've got to be suspicious of someone who believes his own bullshit. Kay and Father Pat are always getting Mum to talk and it's doing her no good. I don't like Kay. I just don't. Maybe it's because Mum is so fond of her.

She's got dark curly hair and wears glasses that make her green eyes larger. She's got an absolutely huge arse; you'd think she must be carrying someone else's as well as her own. Morris said it's wrong to say she has a big arse, it sounds cruel, just call it a big wipe.

Women like to over-emphasise things – if it's not their breasts it's their hair, if it's not their height it's something else, like their fine house, their beautiful clothes – and are capable of sticking little arrows of spite in each other. Sometimes Aunt Julie threw them at Mum, in the form of saying she'd never have kids, never get herself into the money troubles Mum had, talking about her latest holiday, asking Mum to go, knowing she wouldn't. By way of accident, showing Mum her full purse. She was kind, no doubt. But as far as I'm concerned, no one's arse is ever truly clean in this world, and people who act like theirs are are the worst sort to meet.

Morris looks at me when he sees the shotgun in my room. I was awaiting the arrival of a new wardrobe. He has a sheen of fear in his eyes. A good job he didn't see the red cartridges or he'd have rightly flipped. I found a box of them on top of Dad's wardrobe as I was edging it from the wall. Mum wanted the wardrobe burned, saying it was riddled with woodworm. It wasn't. She just wanted it burned. She and the girls felt better for having burned everything belonging to Dad and Adam. Morris said they'd love cremations.

The shotgun's a two-barrel Baikal, and Dad bought it to shoot the dogs that worry the sheep. Adam told me about shooting the dogs, how their eyes stayed open when blood spouted from a hole behind their ear, and how sometimes the spread of bullet cut through their flesh and bone, leaving them lying around in bits on the grass. He said shooting dogs was better than laying poison, because poison killed innocent dogs, and though the noise of the shotgun report and the harm it did wasn't pretty, he always felt the dog got what it deserved. All you had to do to convince yourself was go look at the torn lambs. He said the worse sight he ever saw was a dead lamb halfway out of its equally dead ewe, killed by a pack of dogs from a nearby estate.

Frank told Dad a story about dogs in the Lebanon. He and Dad were half-pissed from the cheap whiskey

Frank brought back from that quare place, sitting in the kitchen, at the table, like best buds. He was Post Commander at some place I can't pronounce, but there'd been problems with stray hounds in the village, and the locals were worried in case they bit someone. Rabies, Frank said. Rabies was a big problem out there. Anyway, he went in the jeep and disposed of a few dogs – miserable-looking creatures for the most part, gone bony, all ribs and mickey, except for two black Labradors, fine-looking animals – but anyway, long story short, he said, that night the captain held a dinner for the local Mucktar, the village chief, in the barracks. The Mucktar fella wanted to run a wire from the barrack generator to his new house, but the captain was having none of it – but he wanted to let him down gently.

'We must discuss what you brought me here to discuss,' the Mucktar fella says.

The captain says, 'Sure … about the gen.'

A wave of hand, 'I thought you invited me here to tell me why my prize dogs were shot.'

Frank said he got connected up to the genny.

The soldier alarm clock bugles. Getting dressed, I knock on Morris's door. He grumbles he is awake. But he isn't fully awake. His door is locked, so I suppose seeing me with the shotgun frightened him more than I thought. He should realise that the gun is safer in my room than anyone else's. Does he forget that Gina's gone for it before, that Adam, too, had thought of using it? Yes, safer in my room. I wouldn't use a gun unless it was a case of extreme emergency. I've seen the damage it can do. Dad let me fire it a couple of times. I shot a dog. It left a big bloody hole in its head. I'd wanted to see the things Adam saw, to experience that moment he said was great, life or death, the answer given in the squeeze of a trigger. I thought it strange that the dog was running along one moment, and wasn't the next. Was dead, its eyes open, like it didn't believe it was dead.

'I'm coming,' Morris says.

'Frank's waiting.'

He isn't, but Morris is so lazy these mornings. He says when he wakes up he feels as if a cloud had been sitting on his face all night. Sometimes he cries in his sleep. He told me that I do that too. I wonder if we share the same bad dreams.

Dreams about Adam walking into the kitchen, saying it was all a big joke. Dreams of Adam trying to fix Mum's cuckoo clock. Of Adam walking into Gina's room, and telling her things will be fine. Looking at Karen in a strange way, a way a brother shouldn't look at a sister. Adam holding Dad's hand. Best of friends, eating cake. Smoking roaches. And Mrs Travis in the background eating an apple, saying losing her eye was the best thing that ever happened to her, next to losing her mind, that is.

Mum's up, grilling sausages. The kitchen smells of burned toast tinged with turf smoke from the range.

'Go easy – Eric's just after going off. Gina was up all night with him.'

I go easy. It's an effort. The radio's on low. Soft music. Mum has showered, trying to drive the lack of sleep from her bones. Kay Walsh is coming today. Mum always makes an effort to clean herself up. She knows Kay will get on to her if she doesn't take care of herself.

'Leave me the key to your room,' Mum says.

I wonder if Morris has told her about the shotgun.

'Yeah, okay.' Nothing to hide, I slide it across the table to her empty cereal bowl, along with a suspicious look. I didn't give her the key to my new wardrobe, where I keep the gun, because she didn't ask me for it.

Morris is in the bathroom. He spends a lot of time in there. Looking at himself. Once I heard him talking to himself in the hall mirror. Telling himself he'll get a nose job done when he grows up, that if a guy could lose his balls and become a woman then a few inches could be lobbed off a nose. His nose isn't that big, it's broad and flat like a boxer's – nostrils like twin caves. I wouldn't advise Morris to take up boxing. God only knows how his nose would turn out.

'Mum?'

'Yes?'

'What did Adam say in his letter?'

Mum's crawl to the cuckoo clock. She scratched her temple. 'Nothing.'

'He wrote nothing – how did he write that – would it be n ... o ... t ...?'

'Victor – shut it! You'll see the letter when I think you should see it and not before then, right?'

'Yeah, right. Okay. But don't think for one minute I'm going to see any counsellor. The only one round here needs to see a counsellor is you, and that other fucker you married.'

Mum's lips harden. I don't care. I don't give one penny fuck what she does to me. She can throw me around the place. Box me blue. I just don't care.

Morris comes in, mumbling good morning, and sits in at the table. His pale-blue eyes only beginning to waken, brightening up on hearing Frank's jeep shaking the cattle grid's loose bars.

I am and I amn't looking forward to getting away for a few days. I like Frank, I don't know why, but I think it's mainly because Adam liked him.

Mum puts what I said behind her and makes a fuss, as if our going is a mini-death for her. Morris climbs into the back of the jeep, as though it is natural for him to take a back seat in everything. The skies are blue, with just a couple of stone-coloured clouds over the Wicklow Mountains. Morris is awful quiet in himself.

We leave the plains behind with its army of sheep and strings of horses coming to and from the gallops. Blue-blanketed horses with white socks belong to Tom, Frank says. I see glimpses of Tom's BMW parked behind the furze. He stands beside the car, his hands buried in his jacket pockets, the one with the dirty-looking sheepskin collar. Frank chats about where we are going, what we'll be doing, smoking as he drives. Then, hitting his mobile, he tells Tom to tell the lad on

Fancy Lad to get his finger out. I don't recognise the grey horse. He looks really well in himself. Perhaps we all need to get away from our house.

'What's the matter, Morris?' Frank says, taking in the rear-view mirror.

'Mrs Travis is out of the home.'

Whisking my head about, I say, 'You're sure?'

'Yeah. Sitting out in her garden, reading a newspaper.'

'Did she see us?'

'I don't think so … she was too busy turning the paper the right way round.'

Frank stops at a set of red traffic-lights. 'There are wonderful drugs for mad people these days. Convinces them and everyone else that they're not mad at all. But God help the lot of us if they run out of that anti-mad drug. And you know something else?'

'What?' I say.

'Wouldn't you just pity someone who takes twice as long to read a paper as us, eh?'

'Yeah,' Morris agrees. He says it in a low, bored voice to show that Frank's effort at being humorous isn't so hot.

The thing with Frank is that he treats us as though we are ten-year-olds. Anti-mad drugs! He'd want to fast-forward his ideas. We're almost fourteen years old. And have come through a lot of shit. We're not kids.

I light up one of his cigarettes. He doesn't know what to say, but he knows what to do. Slapping it out of my wrist he snaps, 'Not in my company, you don't. Cheeky little fucker.'

'You smoke, don't you? You're always smoking.'

'I'm an adult. Wait till you're one. And don't bullshit me. I'm taking youse away for a few days to give Milly a break, so if you think anything of her, don't flute around. Right?'

We pull over in Moate for lunch and then he brings us to Clonmacnoise. The sun washes silvery on the Shannon and the old ruins make me feel how short a time I have on earth, without shortening it of my own accord.

We get Frank talking about Lebanon. He says the love of his life is there, living in Beirut. Her name's Fatima and she teaches at the American University. I don't want to listen to this shit, about love. I want to hear about the time he was shot at by the Hezbollah. But he doesn't want to talk about that, just rubs the shoulder he broke when he dived into a wadi to dodge bullets that sung as they passed him. So he claims.

Morris loves stories. I think he takes them in and then adds his own ingredients to make them exciting.

'The Fatima one ... is she pretty?' he asks.

'One ... Jesus, lads ... she's not a one. Yeah ... long black hair, thin as anything, and a very pleasant personality.'

'Nicer-looking than Detta?' I say. I want him to think of Detta.

His eyes go small, squeezed in by the lines about them. 'I never compared them.'

'No?' I say, letting the doubt drip.

Us

He says nothing, just glances at me, measuring me up for something. Then we see Dildo Magee passing us. He is in his dad's car, with his sister, China, in the back. Dildo pulls a face and gives us a wave. He must be going to visit his mum in the dry out clinic in Athlone. He used to be my best friend up until a year ago. Mum didn't like him coming over to the house and said he was a bad influence. She said this because he bought a naked rubber woman using his mum's credit card. He said he never got to use her because his Mum caught him in bed with her, and stabbed her with his Swiss Army knife. I meant to tell Mum – I thought of it the way you think of things but then forget them – that a rubber woman has no feelings and that, if anything, Mum should have thanked Dildo for giving her a brilliant idea – she should have bought Dad one or two.

Then no one would have got hurt.

Morris has no interest in history, unless it's got to do with cowboys and Indians, so he isn't keen on Athlone Castle and what Frank has to say. He keeps looking at the boats on the Shannon and in the end says he is going to own a boat someday. Then he asks Frank did he know the Indians stuck an arrow in General Custer's penis and stripped all the 7th Cavalry naked when they were dead? Frank says he didn't know. Asks who told him that. Morris says he read it in a book in the library. I say it's shite.

Frank says war is worse than what you would ever read in a book or see in a movie. I say that's shite too.

Robinson Crusoe is my favourite book. I like the idea of being on an island away from everyone. The only thing to watch out for are the cannibals that visit the island now and then. In real life there's cannibals everywhere, looking to eat you from the ankles up. Soul and all. Rats; I read somewhere that there are rats on desert islands. Loads of them. It seems you just can't get away from rats. In my nightmares they've all got faces like Dad and Adam.

Frank rings Uncle Tom in the evening from Westport. They're excited about the grey horse, Fancy Lad, who had flown on the gallops that morning. It's as though the horse is thriving on being away from the farm. Frank tells him that Milly is trying to sell up the house and farm and that we might all benefit from the move.

That'll mean Mum'll have to talk with Dad. He rang a week ago. Looking for her. All businesslike. He thought I was Morris. I know this, because I called him a bastard and he said, 'Morris, you little fucker, put her on to me – or I'll fucking break your little arse when I get a hold of you.'

I hung up. I didn't tell Morris. He's enough on his mind. Anyway, I'm sure the bastard will call again. I'm sure we're all going to see him again. It's only a matter of time.

It's raining so we don't camp out. Frank put us up in a creepy old house in Westport. Morris keeps pestering me all night, every creak of stairs drawing from him a whispered 'Did you hear that?'

Us

He isn't as brave as he likes everyone to think.

Frank comes in at about three in the morning. Smelling the room up with drink and his socks. Mum said their mother would never wash his socks – they were too dirty, as though every bad smell in him leaked out through his soles.

Over breakfast Frank says we will enjoy the climb up Croagh Patrick, where the saint fasted for forty days and banished the snakes from Ireland. He says we are to forget about the prayer stuff and just concentrate on the climbing.

It's tough going in parts, especially now as we near the top. At the summit people flash their cameras. They look like starbursts. The view of Clew Bay is brilliant. An army helicopter hovers almost at its mouth, just where the land runs out. It appears as though they're searching for a body. A few minutes later they fly by the side of the mountain. I wonder if they found anyone. It starts to rain.

The rain doesn't let up, drops as large as bullets. The mountain peak sheets itself in cloud. Frank says it is too dangerous to continue. We make our way down, picking our steps, slipping more than once on the shiny rocks. Morris continually looks behind at the clouds, hoping his silent prayers reach the summit. His prayers are probably the same as mine – mainly for Mum – and for the memory-slate to be wiped clean of its bad parts.

Some things stay in my mind. Awful things. I wonder how it is that Dad could be so kind one minute, like a real dad, and then turn around and be evil. Plain evil.

Dad coming in very late at night, hands reaching under the bedclothes, touching, his breathing hard and full of beer. Leaving me still feeling dirty. Always dirty. It only happened on one night, and he didn't go near Morris. He farted in his sleep. And Dad said he was a dirty little runt, going for me instead. If I thought what he did to me was bad, then Adam's story was worse. He told me on the hill – over a roach he sucked at, his eyes far away – what Dad had done to him.

The following morning I asked Mum to get Uncle Frank to put a bolt on the door. Mum did it herself. I told her I suspected Morris was sleepwalking. Not a bad excuse from a seven-year-old. Some nights later the door handle was lowered and the door shoved against but he never came into our room again. I like to think my daytime scowls kept him away but it probably had more to do with Morris being in the same room as me, and the fact that Gina and Adam were there for him. Maybe Karen too.

A bit of me is angry with Mum. She should have known, should have suspected. Something. Then perhaps she is blind to that sort of thing. Suspected him of doing a lot, being bad, but not that bad. Not a right bad fucker, whose guts I hate, whose face I'd like to spit on, who I'd like to see wriggling in Hell for putting his hands on me, for destroying Adam, for fucking up Gina, Mum. Us all.

And only God knows who else. Perhaps there are others whose lives he's destroyed. Lives we know nothing about. Lives put out in some other mad woman's fucking orchard.

Hell is probably like the Aillwee Caves in the Burren, when the tour guide turns out the light and you see jet-black, and smell nothing only cave dampness and the woman next to you, her sweat coming through her perfume. The lights coming on and Frank telling us to hurry, because he didn't like caves, the sensation of being buried alive. Taking us on to Galway. Knackered tired. Frank trying to pump us of our thoughts, asking questions in a soft tone that isn't natural for him, like a dog trying to miaow – it would raise anyone's suspicions. We tell him little because we don't want to talk with him about Dad or Gina or any of that stuff, because he is Mum's brother and we think she might have put him up to this and he will tell her everything we said. And no one is going to know that when Dad does show his face I am going to take it clean away. And like the dog he shot, his eyes won't believe he's dead, and then I'll shoot myself too, easy peasy; but I haven't finished that part of the plan, yet.

All I have to do is keep my temper in check, lead none of them to suspect that I'm going to kill Dad or myself. A sticking-point with me is that he might die too quickly. Not suffer enough. Like I say – I wouldn't shoot anyone unless it was an emergency. I can't think of any emergency bigger than this. Shooting is better than hanging. It's quicker if messier. That is what Adam told me. He chose not to leave a mess.

We drive on from the caves, up a long and winding road. The sun's out now, the road drying up.

'Ye'll love Galway, lads, ye will. We'll book into the hotel and go for a feed, and get on the rides in Salthill, the go-karts, eh?'

'Great,' Morris says.

'When's the horse running?' I say, putting enthusiasm into my voice, and some apology too for making him think of Detta yesterday.

'Tomorrow … we'll go home rich, boys.'

Morris asks Frank what he means by rich. Frank says he will put a fiver on for us at six to one. Thirty quid.

Morris says he has a poor notion of being rich.

I ask him a question then, and know right away that I shouldn't have. I asked him if he ever shot anyone – a person, not a dog – and if he did, how long did it take him to die.

He doesn't answer. He makes to a couple of times but the words don't form. He and Morris – their eyes are full of silent and troubled questions.

5

Frank

1979

The year I met Detta, the year I joined the army, I'd
been going with her sister, Amy. Detta must have been
about fourteen back then, no more, but she looked even
younger. I was three years older. A gang of us left from
the parish church in Kildare, part of a convoy of vehicles
heading down to Galway to see the Pope. We left early.
Kris Kristoffersen sang his Convoy song on the radio.
I'd been on the piss the night before and had a sick head,
but I was serious about Amy, if not about the Pope, and
definitely not about religion, and wanted to please her.

It was good craic on the way down. The bus driver
was a crazy old guy called Jimmy Dunn, who was gay,
and he had brought his gay companion, Marty Dobbs,
along with him. They didn't speak two words to each
other until we had passed through Portlaoise, and then
Marty asked Jimmy if he had put out the cat. Jimmy said
nothing, just flicked the wipers to clear the windscreen
of midges.

'Did you, Jimmy?' Marty said. He had an effeminate voice.

'I forgot.'

'You forgot? You're always fucking forgetting.'

'Sure, he's your job anyway, you're the one who wanted to get in a cat, not me. I didn't want a cat. I never wanted a fucking cat.'

'I asked you, Jimmy, to put him out. And *you* said *you* would … well, here's one who won't pick up his cat-shit. You can bet your life on it. He'll have all the fecking cushions torn too, fecking shredded. Me mother's cushions.'

Then someone from the back asked if the cat was a surrogate pussy and the bus fell quiet. Funny the things you remember. I remember Detta. She was beautiful but very young. I felt much older than her, and yet there was only three years between us. We looked at each other for a long time and something sparked.

The Pope landed in a red helicopter. It was a grey day, cool and misty. Songs were belted out and a general sense of euphoria lasted throughout the ceremony, and the Pope was great, gave his spiel about the evil of materialism, which we all listened to but forgot, if not immediately, then later on. I caught sight of Julie and Milly making their way to the carpark. Milly was with Mike, Julie walked a bit behind them, with her arms folded, her eyes on the ground, in deep thought.

I thought of these things in the hotel, after checking on Victor and Morris in their double room, farther up the corridor. They've enjoyed the few days – the climb up Croagh Patrick (we couldn't reach the summit because cloud covered cloud and I thought it too dangerous to proceed), the caves – and Leisureland in Salthill crowned things for them. They've had a rough time of it lately. We all have; first Julie, then Adam, and that evil bad fucker, Mike. Jesus, I didn't think shit could rain on the one family so much, but it has, is, and will for the immediate future.

'Young people of Ireland, I love you.' The Pope's words.

Said by the wrong man and it reads like a paedophile's anthem. And that's what Mike is. You wouldn't think it. You would not. I thought he was a sound man, and then I began to notice how unhappy Milly was, and when Julie told me about him hitting her, and how long it was going on for, I called around with Tom to sort out the matter. Julie made sure to have Milly out of the way and the kids were in school. Mike was in the shed, the long shed he used to keep the old tractor and bits and pieces of broken-down cars in. He took these flagaries, off-the-cuff notions, and at this time he was into fixing cars and selling them on – if not that he was at the wrought-iron work, but everything he did fell a little way from being right. His work bore the hallmark you associate with second-hand clothes, slightly soiled or rejected. Around that time his younger brother called. A skinny man with a fine thatch of fair hair, who looked nervous in himself. I got the impression either he owed Mike something or vice versa. Ed, I think his name was.

'What's the problem, lads?' Mike said, shutting the lock, a large heavy-duty piece with a combination. He didn't wait for an answer. He looked jumpy in himself. He said there were rats inside and he had laid poison, lots of it, oats dyed blue, which the rats would eat and become thirsty and when they slake their craving for water they burst. Simply burst.

I told him the problem.

He was a stocky man with thick fingers, the dirt rich under his thumbs.

'Yeah, I hit her … but she deserved it.'

I used to be naive and think that all women-beaters were weak and craven cowards, but Mike wasn't a coward and there was no fear in his eyes.

'Deserved it?' Tom said.

I put a hand up straight, like a traffic cop does to stop traffic behind him. Tom was strong but he has a weak chin and a weaker stomach. He stopped against my outstretched arm.

'And she is my wife, and it's none of your business what goes on in my family.'

'She's my sister,' I said.

'And the two of you have come to tell me that, is that so – her big brothers. Mighty men, huh? In my hole.'

'Just me, Mike.' I stood back. He drew his hand under his nose, and went to walk past me.

'Get the fuck off my property,' he spat.

I headed him across the bridge of the nose and followed it with an elbow to his chest. I hit him so hard and so many times he looked nothing like himself when I was finished. And as he lay there, groaning and spitting out an eye-tooth, I said, 'I brought Tom along just to pull me off you – next time he stays at home. Understand? One finger on Milly and you'll be looking for a jamjar to hold your balls.' If I'd known then what I know now I'd have kept on beating him and fed his nuts to the crows.

I'm Adam's godfather. I wasn't one in name only. I got to see a lot of the kid. I saw him in the Rotunda the day he was born, a wrinkled-up little thing in Milly's arms. I bought him presents and brought him places as he grew older. All the time I didn't know that Mike was destroying his kids' lives.

Adam's the one who sat on my knee in Julie's house – he must have been only eight when Detta and me split – and said, 'Don't be sad, Frank, you'll find someone else, and you've got all of us.'

When I got the news, I was in Beirut seeing Fatima while on a sixty-hour leave pass from my unit. She's an older woman. A lusty beauty who lives in an apartment not far from the American University. She works in a bookshop for an old Armenian writer who moved his family from Lebanon during the Civil War and lost all touch with them. In less than a year I qualify for my army pension and hope to settle in Beirut with Fatima, and see how things go. That's the plan. I don't know how earnest we are about it. It's putting more distance between me and Sam, my son.

Drink broke my marriage. Outwardly, to many people, that is the case. They say I'm a header with the beer in me. But I can quit. I quit for a month or so each year before I head over to see Detta and Sam. I have the slightest of trembles in my hands and Detta is quick to pick up on things. The weight's gone off me and I've got a bony look. I eat fags. Eat them. The army doctors are at me to cut back on them a little and then give them up entirely. But it's not just the drink that shagged things up for me. Something else played its part and I didn't know for a long time what it was, and I don't think anyone else did, either.

The lads are okay, a little subdued. I think they had a row with each other. They're watching a late movie. Back in my own room I draw the curtains and keep the lights off, uncork a bottle of wine and sit with it in front of the window. The stars burn brighter over Lebanon.

It was late 1985, almost Christmas. I was stationed in Tyre, a port city about twenty-four kilometres from the Israeli border. A city full of Phoenician, Greek, Roman, Crusader and Byzantine ruins. A city where the rotting corpses of dogs glistened under sun and sea spray on fine white beaches, where boy soldiers prowled the streets like a wind you couldn't say which way was blowing. We got a radio call in the patrol car to proceed to a traffic accident on the coastal road, near Checkpoint Two Dash Four. The checkpoint had x-shaped tank-stops and spike-rails but that didn't stop the killers. They drove up to the post and shot two Fijian soldiers dead. Joe, the Lance Corporal with me, knew them. They were guys due to rotate home the following week, after spending a year away from home.

Numb, that's how I felt, and sickened too. The smell of oranges and lemons from the groves were fresh and mingled with the heavy, thick smell of blood. The first soldier lay face down outside his pillar box, his helmet had fallen off because a bullet took it clean away, along with half his chin. The UN stencil markings on the helmet had faded (amazing how you remember small details). The other chap took two rounds to his chest, through the opened Velcro stitching on his blue flak jacket. He was a barrel-chested man and the jacket was too small for him. It wouldn't have saved his life even if he could have closed it up.

I remember the flies lighting on the blood and the two men carted away, their blood washed off on the streets, the rain becoming more substantial. Seeing death like that, up close, the shock in a dead man's eyes, the hole in his face, the one in his back, you think how it could be you and that's a shameful part of how I used to feel. I felt weak and vulnerable. All sorts of everything preyed on my mind; I became morose and irritable, and started having sleepless nights. That's the spanner that loosened the nut on my marriage – the drink was just another tool that turned other nuts. I'm grand now. But it took time, and, funnily enough, more trips abroad to cure me or cope – cope's probably more accurate. The drink did its part, but it's overstayed its welcome. I've got to do something about quitting. And I will. Sometime.

Burying Adam brought it all back. Seeing him lying in his coffin, and thinking about his wasted life. Not a mark on him. *Not a mark we could see.* Holding Milly, I cried my eyes out. Losing Julie was bad enough, but bad as it is, you accept disease and accidents as sad yet natural – it's the way the cards fall. They say Adam killed himself, but I think he was murdered. Yeah, he jumped, fitted the noose around his neck, but that's not what I'm talking about. Mike may as well have done these things to him and finished off the job he started. As far as I'm concerned, he picked the cards Adam had to play with.

I get to bed about two, leaving three glasses in the bottle just to prove that I can, and reach some level of sleep not entirely restful.

I wake early, listen to morning noises, birds, and the first murmurs of traffic, basking in the shaft of sun falling in through the window. Sleepily, I take up my mobile and call Milly. She answers quickly.

'Frank here, Milly.'

'Frank … great, how are the boys?'

'No problem … I'm bringing them racing today, then we should be back about eightish this evening.'

A pause.

'Is everything all right, Frank?'

Another pause.

'Yeah, Milly … I just called, you know?'

I hear her sigh of understanding.

'I know, Frank … thanks.'

She goes on to say that Detta had sent a card. It has Goofy on the front. She's marrying this fella she's been dating for a while and wants us over for the wedding. We're on friendly terms but not that friendly. The guy's name is Fred Tex and he's a rugged mountain of a man, non-drinker, non-smoker, and into lifting weights. He comes across as Mister Perfect. Sam goes on and on about him and while it irks, I say nothing. I only see him for two weeks every year and so I'm not going to give him bad memories of me, or turn him against Detta or Fred Tex. Besides, it's good to see he likes his *new father,* and that they get along with each other. There isn't the friction that existed between Mike and his kids. A heightened tension created by fear and distrust … probably hatred.

I'd needed to call Milly. I worry about her all the time. So does Tom. I live with Tom – not in his cottage, though, but in a mobile home on a site he gave me. It's new, and rests on bricks and has a wooden veranda. It has two bedrooms and works on gas for heating and cooking and for supplying hot water. It's in better shape than Tom's place. He has a new woman in his life called Geraldine, a nice woman, compared to his wife.

Jesus. I was away on duty one night, and when I came home she was gone. Nance. Poor fucked-up Nance.

Tom had been away too, at an evening race meeting in Roscommon. When he came home she said she'd something to tell him. I found him in his sitting-room, holding his head in his hands. He was crying.

'Tom?'

He looked at me. I knew that look. I saw it in the mirror when Detta left me.

He told me Nance said she'd slept with someone while he'd been away. She'd met him in town. He spoke a lot, Tom did, that morning, that afternoon, and we drank a couple of bottles dry, and we talked deep-talk and light-talk, and wondered what the fuck was wrong with us, because we lost wives the way some people lost shirt buttons.

'Know what, Frank, know the worst possible thing – the worst *possible* thing?'

He was almost out of it, so drunk he just wanted to sleep.

'What?'

'It … it took me two years to get a – get a – feel of her diddy, and that – that other fucker got the whole lot in one night.'

We breakfast about eight. The boys are grumpy. Especially Victor. He has a certain way of looking at people – I don't like it. Glassy eyes that'd cut you quick as a blade. Morris smiles now and then but I haven't seen Victor smile … I can't remember the last time I did.

Morris says, 'Where are we meeting Uncle Tom?'

Victor cuts in, 'Where do you think, Dummy – on the Moon? At the racecourse.'

'Victor! Give it over, sip up your orange and try to be nice. Yeah, Morris, at the racecourse. In about an hour.'

Tom meets us with bad news. He stands outside the stable looking over the half-door at Fancy Lad. Right off, I expect to find that the horse is dead in the box. I find it's for the best to think the worst, that way it lessens the shock, keeps you from panicking.

Tom shakes his head, 'I've pulled him out.'

'Why?'

I sense the boys' disappointment.

'Because...' Tom takes us all in, 'because I entered him in a colt and fillies race, that's the why.'

It doesn't click with me for a few moments and the boys' faces wear puzzled expressions.

'Fancy Lad has no goolies. He's a gelding but I've no record of it. I was poxed to find out. If I'd have run him I might have lost my licence.'

'How did you find...?'

'A woman who knows her horses and their parts told me. I owe her a drink.'

After the race meeting, Tom gallops Fancy Lad against a horse from another stable, coming in behind the chestnut by four lengths. The boys aren't impressed, but I am. Tom had told the young fella aboard Fancy Lad to hang back, not to show his hand. Tom has a winner all right in Fancy Lad. It is just saved for another day.

He hasn't declared Mike as the owner, nor Milly, just using the initial M in front of Nugent because Mike is officially listed as the owner. Milly's. The horse is Milly's as far as we're concerned. Not that I think Mike will come back to kick up a fuss. But he might. If the horse wins it will kill him to think we put one over on him.

6

Gina

September

The smell. It meets us on the outskirts of Kildare Town and makes me feel as though I walked on dog dirt. I forgot about that smell, the way it cruised through Aunt Julie's sash windows, forcing us to feed the bin with our dinners. Amazing how some factory smells close your stomach.

I tell Mum I'd prefer to wait in the car while she goes to the AIB Bank. She says she'll meet me in Boland's for lunch, and I nod and say okay. The smell is gone, dying somewhere on the Curragh Plains, amongst the furze and raths, but I'm not hungry. These days I'm never hungry, these days I'm constantly tired, these days I just don't care about anything any more.

I sit in the car and look at the people through the dirt-streaked windscreen. Mum had tried the wiper wash on the way in, but it was empty. Dad always made sure little things like that worked.

I feel dirty, dirty all over. A baby, mine. At my age. Sixteen. Jesus. I only know one other girl who had a baby at that age. She was in my class. I've often seen her around with the baby's father. He's black, the baby's black, and sometimes they draw black scowls of disapproval from people. I can't knock around with the father of my baby. He isn't here. And, I don't go out much, because people know what happened, and they look at me in a certain way, making me feel that the dirt has suddenly become visible.

I confirmed that I was pregnant by using a pregnancy testing kit. When the stuff turned blue, I freaked. I didn't tell anyone for a long time, then I mentioned it to Dad, after he entered my room for his Friday Night Right as he said. He made a joke out of doing what he did. I knew it was wrong. So wrong. But he'd been doing it for years and I didn't know how to stop him. He gave me more pocket money than he gave the others. A reward for being a good girl, he said. I was cheap. A home-grown ride. I hate his fucking guts.

I was little when he started, sitting me on his knee, touching me all over. Smothering me with himself. His eyes hot for me. His fingers reminded me of snakes, except I'd always thought that snakes would feel cold, slimy, and mushy. These snakes sweated, and felt bony on my flesh.

'Pregnant?' he said, sitting on the edge of my bed. A cold March wind was on the rise. I could have screamed at him, but I never did. A scream would have had Mum come running, and Karen, and the lads. But it was far too late to scream for help. The secret, his *right,* was as much my secret as his. Probably more mine than his.

It was in my interest to keep quiet. In the first place, I didn't want to hurt Mum, I didn't want people looking at me, I didn't want anyone to know. I tried to hide the dirt. But you can't hide dirt. Not forever, not even with baggy jumpers.

'You can't be,' he said. 'No way.'

'I am.'

'You're sure?'

'I did the test – what am I going to do?'

He said nothing for a few moments, looked at the wedding band on his finger, sucked in his cheeks, made a grinding noise with his teeth. His breath smelled of mint, the rest of him of Brut. Ordinarily, he'd be lying on top of me, taking his right. And I would close my eyes, and pretend he was George Michael, or one of Take That, or Boyzone. Any of them, all of them. It made things easier. In my mind's eye he was anyone but my father.

'Who else was at you?' he said, in a low voice.

I looked away. What did he want me to say? The room filled with ice. I wanted to ask him who else *he'd* been at. Adam told me. So, I knew. And I felt very afraid of Dad, for he was very strong, and I often felt he could kill someone, and when I thought about what he'd done to me and Adam, I knew that people like him are capable of doing anything. At you ... at you. Say it quickly enough, and it sounds like a sneeze.

79

'Who else?' he snarled.

'No one.'

A silence between us, the wind noisy, disturbing a tin can out the back – ghosts playing football – or trying to reach us?

He hit me then, across the face. It stung. I felt a trickle of blood. It tasted sweet. Grabbing my hair, wrapping it around his hand he pulled me towards him. He said, 'It's not me who's the daddy. Remember that.'

Then he got up and left, easing the door shut behind him. He had a practised way of closing the door. I sat there, tears streaming down my cheeks. In the dark, the taste of salty tears on my tongue replacing the one of blood.

I read somewhere in a newspaper an article about child abusers. Except I wasn't really a child, and I didn't look on Dad as being an abuser. I couldn't put a name like that on him. It makes what he did appear ordinary, or something … I think something like 'life ruiner' sounds better. At first I thought all daddies did what he did. I thought it was an extension of his love for me. I thought he was normal, which for the most part he came across as being.

He spoke with and laughed with people. He worked on committees. He had definite opinions about things. He didn't speak in a soft, slimy voice that would make him easy to dislike, would make him fit the picture of an abuser. Someone who was easy to hate.

Us

I was doing very well in school, expected to go places, the best in my class by a clear mile in most subjects. All I had to do, the teachers said, was to continue working, and success would follow. I worked, I loved studying.

None of them warned me about becoming pregnant. They probably thought I was too bright for such a thing to happen, and that I wasn't the sort to hang around with boys. I bet they got a shock. I bet I was a big disappointment to them.

His shadow was long and dark, as shadows are. There are different kinds of shadows. Some are hand-movements done on walls to amuse children, of a dog, a rabbit, other animals less well done. More are lengths and widths of ourselves exaggerated by the sun. Shadows we stomped on when we played our children's games. And there are other shadows unseen by the human eye, which, though invisible, have a presence more real, and, oh God, much more harmful. Far-reaching shadows with black-tipped secrets to chill and shame the bravest of hearts, which live deep within some of us, released only by pain of death. Ask Adam.

Once, I saw Dad crying over pictures of starving children in Africa, and saw him write out a cheque there and then. He wasn't a monster like the papers paint such people, nor was he entirely evil. Small peeps of goodness came through in him, but the skies sealed forever when I told him I was going to have a baby. He started looking at Karen. I don't think he ever touched her. I wasn't sure, then. We're not really close to each other, the way some sisters are. I got along better with Adam, we'd more in common.

I thought about having an abortion. Sometimes I wish I had it done. But I couldn't sneak out the door and just disappear. I didn't know where to go and I'd no money. Fifty pounds in my Post Office book, that's all. I told Karen first. I don't know why I did. But I had to tell someone, and Adam ... I just couldn't tell him, not then, at first. The twins were too young to involve in this. And yet, there was no way for them to avoid being involved.

Karen touched between her legs, as though she had suddenly got sick there. Her face scrunched up. She looked up at the clear blue sky. The air was fresh and smelt of heather, bracken, furze, and rain-soaked bog. We stood not far from the house, halfway up a slight incline in a field of purple-tipped thistles.

'Dad?' she said, her eyes popping.

'Didn't he ever touch you?'

'No – you're sick, Gina. He wouldn't....'

I yelled at her. There was no one about. A tractor murmured past in the next field. A cow bellowed in sympathy with me. Karen stood there, in her best jeans and low-cut blouse, shaking her head, and I knew then she believed me, and knew then that she'd lied. Dad had touched her, and when I got it out of her, she said he'd never gone the full way, that she had cried too much for his liking. We sat in the field, holding hands. Near us flies buzzed on sun-baked cowpats and we cried. About as close as we would ever get.

I don't know how I conjured up the name Terry Magee. I was so brave, had hyped myself up to tell Mum, but at the very last second changed my mind and Terry Magee was born. I wish giving birth to Eric had been as easy. Mum copped on right off. She knows when I'm lying. My face gives me away. At least Dad's gone, and sometimes I think, and I feel fucking awful when I think it, that if Eric were dead, things could come back to normal, or almost normal. There's no way we can be fully normal after what Adam did to himself. A fucking eejit to do what he did – I promised him I wouldn't open my mouth. I told him not to worry. I kept telling him not to worry, over and over, but he just wouldn't listen. I told him Dad was to blame, that that fucker started everything. God, I loved Adam. He was too soft for his own good. Nervous in himself. I'm so fucking mad at him.

I felt like killing myself when I found out I was pregnant. I wanted to take an 'E' and jump in the river, but I hadn't the courage. Courage to kill yourself – it must take a little. But if you want something bad enough, you'll do anything to get it. I guess I didn't really want to die.

I get out of the car. There are moments when I just don't want to be alone with my thoughts. It's a grey day in a grey town. Pubs and more pubs. A really good restaurant and an athletic club Adam joined and ran a few cross country races with, getting thorns in his feet that Mum spent Sunday afternoons freeing, buying him a pair of spikes the week before he packed it in.

Morris plays in goal for the soccer team but hasn't been in to train with them since Adam died. He's a very good goalie, with fast reflexes I didn't think he had because he walks about our place so slowly and does everything else at crawl pace too. Victor's hyper. Sometimes I forget they're twins.

Everyone's been great. Really great. If Aunt Julie were alive she'd be a great help too. I often thought of telling her about Dad, but the opportunity never came my way. I could have phoned, but news like mine shouldn't be dropped on someone by phone. Kay Walsh tries her best, but I catch a little give-away set to her lips when she looks at me. So deep down I think she'd like to give me a root up the arse, even though deep down she knows I'm the victim. Then, maybe it's because she heard I had shaken the shite out of Eric a couple of times. I shouldn't do that, I know, but his crying gets to me. It does. But I don't do it any more. It's hard not to. But his smallness frightens my hands. They all think he looks like Dad, but I don't see him in Eric at all. That's good too. If he looked like that twisted bollocks, I don't think I could ever stop shaking him.

I brought him for a walk the other day in his pram. I met Queenie Travis. She was sitting outside on a bench, reading her paper. She saw me on the road and came over. I was hoping she wouldn't see me. She never shuts up. Karen said she just wanted to eye up Eric. Eye. Funny. Hah, hah. Her glass eye gives me the shudders. Unblinking, and yet I think she can see more with an eye that never shuts down.

'She's gorgeous,' she said in her mild accent.

'How old is she?'

'He's almost four months.'

'I should have known – did I say she – I meant he. Blue for a boy. Yes. Lord God, he's a fine baby. Isn't he just? The size of him. He's well made that fella.'

She smelled as dirty as I felt. She asked me inside but I said no, that it was almost Eric's feeding time and I hadn't brought a bottle. She asked what feed he was on.

'SMA.'

Her lips pursed, 'You can't beat breastfeeding, you know. I was read–'

'Well, when you've small, sensitive tits you go with the bottle.'

Nosy old fart – who did she think she was? Didn't she know that Aunt Julie died from cancer of the breasts? That we're all a little wary of anything got to do with breasts?

Then I remembered she was mad, that she'd been the one to find Adam, who'd gone to cut him down, but couldn't, who'd come up the road waving a knife, her neighbours running after her, trying to stop her screaming. And then I felt sorry for her. She walked up the footpath, her iron gate closing behind her, like a mouth tired of seeing the same food. I took in the brown masking tape on her bedroom window. Someone fired a stone through her window the night Adam died. No one knows who. The guards ruled out anyone being with Adam when he died and put the broken window down to vandalism.

What's Mum looking at in the future? Julie's dead, and Adam returned the life she gave him. Dad's gone, leaving her with bills and a couple of old nags. It pinches my heart, scalds my nerves, when I think of her thinking we both had babies for the same man. I make my way into Boland's and order soup and soda bread. I feel as though people are looking at me, that something to talk about, to break their mundane routine, has walked in on top of them.

It's so hard to believe that Adam is dead, that I have a baby boy. That Aunt Julie is gone. So hard. Sometimes I feel as though I'm going to snap, and other times I just don't care what happens to me, or anyone else. I'd like to go to a rave, pop a couple of 'E' pills and dance myself out of my skull. Forget about everything, the present, the future, but mostly the fucking past. Especially that. Maybe one of these nights I will – myself and Karen will go off on a night out together. But I want to wait until Eric is bigger before I start going out again. I don't like leaving him, even though there are times I wish he wasn't here for me to leave.

Us

If he were a doll I could pick him up and stick him in the closet, leave him there until whenever. But he cries, he shits, he pisses, he eats, he screams, he smiles and laughs. He lets me know he's around. He puts his hands out for me to lift him. And I always do because if I don't I know I would feel bad about it. Is that love, or is it just being prepared to do anything to keep him from crying?

The soup comes over and the bread. I don't know the girl. She smiles. I could be anyone. I tell her my Mum will fix her up when she comes in. She said not to worry. I receive Unmarried Mother's Allowance, but I hand most of it up to Mum. She hasn't any money coming in and I've caught her looking at the job ads in the *Kildare Nationalist*. She's thinking about working in the Stream factory on the Monasterevin Road but the shiftwork doesn't suit her, not at the moment anyway. Her brother Frank is very good to us. I suspect he takes care of the ESB and phone bills and that. Tom leaves in a box of groceries every week. He leaves it at the back door, early in the morning, before any of us are up. No ever talks about what they do, it's charity, and I know Frank and Tom mean well, but Mum has pride, and having to accept charity hurts, hurts her pride a lot.

Frank is Eric's godfather and Kay Walsh is his godmother. I didn't really want her doing it but Mum had her asked before I could say anything, and it wasn't worth causing a row. Father Toner sprinkled the blessed water and said his stuff. He smiled a lot and touched

Eric's soft black hair, making me wince, because it brought back memories of Dad's hand on my head. We had a meal out in the Silken Thomas in Kildare, and Eric got sick on his dribbler, and everyone fussed and in the end they did so much fussing I told them all to fuck off and leave us alone. And the restaurant fell quiet. Quieter still when a little man with twitching muscles in his jaw came over and chewed on us for a minute. But he did it very nicely, not cursing or anything, and in a soft voice. Much like Dad used do when I was little and he was putting his hand inside my knickers.

I can't help thinking that all men are dirty but I know they're not. I've been alone with Frank in his jeep, and with Tom, and they never did anything or said anything out of the way. I remember thinking that they mustn't find me attractive. Imagine thinking like that.

Father Pat arranged a counsellor to see us. At first Mum was keen on the idea, but she's put him on hold because Victor blew his rocket over seeing him and has become very aggressive lately. He's giving Mum a rough time, especially over Adam's letter. He wants to read it. I couldn't be bothered – if he said anything about me I'm sure Mum would have told me by now. Definitely. Victor's changed. He curses a lot, and I've caught him smiling to himself, and nodding his head. Morris, I'd swear that fella doesn't give a shite about anything, only opens his mouth to feed himself. The twins resemble Dad in little ways; they have his look, his crooked smile, they like the same food, the same TV programmes. I don't mind seeing the counsellor. I'd go to the Moon if I thought it'd put an end to me seeing Dad and Adam in small everyday things.

I hate feeling the way I do. Dirty, dirty, dirty. I can never wash myself enough. I keep thinking that I should get away, move out with Eric, but I'd be afraid of hurting him if we were alone. I used to think about leaving him and just going. But I couldn't do that before I had him, to get rid of him, and I'm not leaving him now. That thought hurt too much. I guess deep down I love my baby.

Mum comes in and sighs with relief to see that I hadn't stayed in the car. She sits across from me and asks if the soup is okay, and then orders an egg mayonnaise because she says she has an ulcer on her tongue and the soup will aggravate it. A sore thing, she says, adding that I am to remind her to drop into the chemist and get something for it. It could have been a day a year ago, when I was pregnant but didn't know it, and Dad had just come off me the night before, and Adam complained about the length of time I spent in the shower, and the twins were boxing each other with the gloves Frank bought them, which Mum later threw out because Victor tried to box Morris into oblivion, and was getting angry because Morris was too quick on his feet, and cuffed him a couple of times, and then Victor got the measure of him, and we all thought Morris's nose was broken, and feared his blood wouldn't stop pumping, and that we'd have to bring him to hospital to get his nose straightened, until we realised that Morris's nose wasn't straight to begin with. Victor has caused two bloody noses in our house; Adam's was the other.

'Have you thought about going back to school?' Mum asks.

I shake my head. I used to have long red hair (dyed) but I wear it short now, and I don't worry so much about my big ears.

'You should.'

'Around here … Mum … come on …it's finished for me around here. Finished for me … I just couldn't settle back in.'

'People know it wasn't your fault – and besides, they're too busy getting on with their own lives – everyone has something on their plate to worry about, you know?'

'Not many have this.'

Mum sighs, expelling the little tortures in her.

'Mum … you don't understand. It's finished for me here. I'd feel like a … an untouchable. Who's going to want anything to do with me … what fella will take on a girl who had…?' I stop, because I don't want to breathe his name.

Mum looks at my empty soup bowl, taking sanctuary in the fact that I had eaten something, at last.

'Things will improve,' she says.

'I don't know, Mum …have you seen how aggressive Victor is becoming with each passing day?'

'He'll get it out of his system too. We all will. Somehow.'

Finally, I breathe it, finally, his name, 'Dad…?'

Her features darken like the drawing in of a winter's evening, her lips part, then shut and open again. She says she has taken a call from him. He wants to sell the farm and probably will. The bungalow is half hers and he wants her to agree to sell up. He mentioned a figure to her, that he'd give her if she agreed, so ridiculously low she had to laugh. Then she remembered what he did and the sound of his voice, not what he was actually saying, sickened her, and she slammed down the phone.

'He asked about his horses,' Mum says. 'His horses – no mention of his kids.'

'What about his horses?'

'He says he'll be sending a horsebox round for them. I told him that Tom had taken them to his yard – he went quiet, then sighed – so I said what else did he expect? I had no money to buy feed for them.'

'And what did he say to that?'

'Nothing. Just grunted. I hate the way he grunts. Pigs don't do it so well.'

Mum says that Dad said he doesn't care, he wants his horses back, and that he'll have them stabled elsewhere on the Curragh, probably at the end of month.

'He didn't like it when he heard his horse was entered in a race – he said if it won he wanted the prize money. I had to laugh – I told him I'd lodge it into his bank account.'

She puts the pad of her forefinger to the coffee froth rimming the inside of her mug and breaks its circle. She has a small smile, carrying a punch, 'I don't know where he banks. Never did.'

'Why didn't you know? Jesus, Mum, you're backward. Honestly.'

'He always gave me money, measured it so it would be a drop short of enough – if I asked for more he let on he didn't hear me – he didn't have bank statements coming to the house – so, I mean… yes, backward … you're right … I was slow. Slow in stopping his nonsense in its tracks. In stopping all of his nonsense.'

Nonsense. Mum calls what he did nonsense. A very mild word, Mum, but I let it go. Then, she said, they had it hot and heavy. When Mum said Ned's wife, Annie, had called, he quietened and then asked what did she want. Mum said Ned was missing. Did he know where he was? No! He started up about selling the house then, and wanting to drop by and collect his things. If she could arrange for everyone to be out, just for an hour. He got thick when she said there was nothing of his in the house, and it got heavy again, and then her stomach came at her, over the things he had done, and she shut down on him. Completely. Left the phone off its cradle.

'The pharmacy,' I say to Mum as we pass one on the way to the car.

She checks her stride, and says, 'Yes, I have to get something, your father's breath down the line probably gave me this bloody thing.'

'He is one, Mum, a head-to-toe ulcer.'

We smile entering the shop. The old man behind the counter smiles, too, as though he is happy to see a pair in his shop who don't have a care in the world.

7
Milly

September

Kay arrives in the afternoon, on a sour day with a taste of rain on the wind. It is so, so good to see her.

Earlier that morning I hung clothes on a line that decided to snap, sending my washing to the ground. I picked up the items: smalls, shirts, and sweaters, and put them in the basket. They were destroyed. Just when I thought I was getting a headstart on the day, I had to begin all over, a bit like the sum of my life so far, crisis after crisis. I saw it then, crawling and then stopping to sniff the air, its grey whiskers shivering in the slightly cold Curragh breeze. It was grey with a long tail and I don't know for sure if its eyes were black but I think they were, a polished black, like the toecaps of Frank's parade boots. A rat. It came from the shed Mike used to spend his evenings in; before he left he'd been cleaning it out, selling off the bits and pieces of cars and tractors he kept inside, with the intention of knocking the place down and rebuilding it as a leisure centre. He was a dreamer, always thinking up ways to make money, but never having any real lasting zeal or patience to make anything work. I backed inside, pausing at the rainwater barrel beside the back door, and checked to see if the rat had gone. It hadn't, and there were several more by its side. I felt bile come up my throat, and going inside I locked the doors and told the kids to close all the windows in the house. The twins, Morris and Victor, were away with Frank and I didn't tell the girls about the rats because they would have gone hysterical.

Kay drives a Nissan Micra with a dent in its right wing, and L signs plastered back and front on the windows. I think she must have sat her driving test about five times. She says the next time she's going to wear a short skirt and offer her body to the tester. She's not a bad driver, I think, but she doesn't stop talking. I think that's why she has failed so many times. If she could only keep quiet for the duration of the test.

It made me feel good to see her heading this way. To think we didn't take to each other that first day in Woodcraft when she sat behind her desk, touching her glasses, looking at the boss, John, going through things with me. At one stage he leaned a little too closely for comfort. His clothes smelled of mothballs and I glimpsed some of his fillings. Kay coughed and said, 'John, why don't you get up on her altogether?'

He glared at her and moved off. I knew then they'd a special employer-employee relationship. She's the sort of person who, if she likes you, can't do enough to help. I like the way she listens (she stops talking sometimes). I like the fact that she comes round, and makes me feel she's coming round just because she enjoys visiting. Her brazenness can be off-putting at times, though she always shows me her smooth side. Kay has told me things about herself that I think she's afraid to tell anyone else, even Father Pat. I know she's grown cold on John, has long given up the idea that he might leave his wife. She lives in a small terraced house with her father, who refuses to get in the car with her, who tells her he can't eat the food she cooks.

Kay's into Oriental dishes; her kitchen is full of woks, chopsticks, and menu books. She keeps asking me round to stay for a week or two, and while I know it'd do me good, I can't just walk out on the kids. Although, at times, there's nothing I'd like better in the world than to hear the front door slamming behind me for good, and it's something I intend doing when I get enough money together – but with the kids – I need them.

Kay says that selling the house is a good idea. Pat thinks I should sell up too. I agree with them but it means I'll have to talk with that bastard. The house is in both our names. He signed over my share to me, but that only happened because we remortgaged a few years ago and it was a stipulation in the policy. But he could be so generous, with his time, his money, and yet he could be so cold, flinching at my touch on his arm, needing that extra body space from me, not wanting to be near anyone until he himself gives the okay *or* made it okay. Why did he have to spoil it all? Was he always sick? How many of my kids has he touched? The fucker.

I've asked them all. Except Gina, she doesn't have to answer. Karen shook her head. But I know she's lying, although she's a more convincing liar than Gina. Morris looked at me as though I'd two heads and said nothing. Victor turned on me, wanted to know why I was asking now, why I didn't ask before? Why didn't I?

Thoughts of him lying with Gina, doing the act, make me physically sick. I wonder about the twins. I know about Adam. He told me in his letter. Jesus Christ. Am I blind? Am I naive or just plain stupid? How come I know when my kids are lying and not when they're hurting? Kay and Father Pat can't answer these questions. I can't either. I know he cheated on me. I know that. He was going to Dublin a lot. I asked him about her one day out of the blue. I found something belonging to him in his jacket that I thought needed to see the dry cleaners; a hotel bill, with drinks and minute steaks for two. The kids were in school. We were alone. I asked the question millions of women must have asked their men.

'Who is she?'

He sat in at the table, the paper spread before him. It was early summer, and he wore a check sleeveless shirt. His forearms rippled with cord-like veins. I made out the small heart-shaped tattoo near his wrist, under the fine growth of dark hairs. I saw things in him that morning I'd forgotten about. Lovers' things.

'Angela.'

He looked at me with these eyes I didn't recognise as his. He was in one of his uncaring moods.

'How much?'

'What?'

'You heard, you fucking heard me.'

'Is that all you think I'd shift – a whore? Well, here's news for you, she's not.'

'Why … what are you playing at, Mike?'

I knew better than to lose my temper with Mike, to rail against him, to attack him. I would lose out, the kids would lose out, and Mike would lose out. He has hit me before, infrequently, but the love was in him afterwards. It was as though he had to prove he could hurt me before he could love me. He smothered me with affection, but now that's gone. In its place, blame for the ventures he undertook that didn't pan out, and no praise for the ones that did, and contempt, sheer and utter, pure contempt. He has a look about him that shows people what he thinks of them – a horrid look.

He shrugged, 'She's a great ride.'

I caught my breath. Ride.

'She's funny, isn't bitching all the time. I can relax in her company. I don't feel as if I have to be someone with her, wear my best clothes sort of thing.'

I said nothing. I went cold inside. He never fully matured as a person. Not quite there as your ordinary decent human being. I was hurt, but not as hurt as I would have been had I loved him. I had a benign tolerance of him, for the kids' sake (how sick that sounds now).

'She acts the woman in bed.'

'She must be hard up to have anything to do with you.'

'Angela's a real woman – big tits.'

Now I knew he wanted to rise me.

'She lets me touch her breasts.'

'Touch or maul, she's welcome to your fingers … does she ever tell you to take the sheepshite out from under your nails?'

His cheeks reddened but the anger he felt came out in a derisive smile. I said no more, because Frank was away, and if Mike thought of that he might itch to hit. I got up and moved my things into the utility room. I should have moved out his things but I wanted to shed his presence. His presence lurks, even when he's not about.

I let Kay in. She's brought fresh cream eclairs from Bradbury's Bakery with her. She's putting on weight. As usual, she's smiling.

'The road's busy – Jesus, but Kildare is a terrible town to drive through.'

'I have the kettle on,' I say.

We sit in the kitchen on chairs with split cushions showing us their wounds. Gina nurses Eric on her lap and Karen is in her room. We move into the sitting-room when we need to smoke and have a chat. Gina won't let anyone smoke in front of the baby. They appear to be bonding. I hope so, because I doubt if too many of the rest of us will ever get close to him.

'Did he ring?' Kay asks, drawing on a cigarette, the smoke mingling with the rising steam from her coffee.

'Again, no, he didn't ring. Not yet. God, Kay, I hate the thought of speaking with him.'

'But you'll have to in order to sell the house – you need to get away from here.'

Kay hasn't reminded me, but this is the morning I promised to show her Adam's letter. I'm glad she's not the pushy sort. Father Pat knows what's in it, and perhaps he discussed the contents with her, but I doubt it. That man is rock solid. We talk about everything and it's great to listen to someone who'll talk about other things that happened in the world. It takes the emphasis off your own problems.

'The Queen – I hate her,' Kay says. 'She gave Di a terrible life. Have you got her autobiography? I must give it you when I'm finished reading it. She was a lovely person, too good by far to get mixed up with those Windsors in the first place. And now look, Eddie's getting married….'

I hand her the letter to read. I thrust it at her. I want her to tell me what she thinks.

Her eyes tumble down the red lines. And as she reads I look about the room. The heavy, green drapes, the bird dirt on the window, the floral wallpaper, the ash cold in the fireplace, its marble hearth cracked and chipped at the corners. Adam played in here with his toy soldiers, stood behind me handing me Christmas tree decorations, laughed when the whole lot fell on me.

It wasn't a room I let them into too often. Kids destroy good furniture. When one was sick I used to lie him on the sofa, cover him with a quilt, bring in the portable TV and buy him comics. The girls, when they were sick, preferred to stay in their own bedrooms, with the smells of perfume and dolls, their music.

I know every word she reads. When I read it I can hear Adam's voice, picture him clearly, so clearly. Picture him making his First Communion in his new clothes. The gap in his teeth showing in a broad smile, freckles about his nose that faded a year later. I'd sell my soul to have five minutes with him, just five fucking minutes.

He missed words in his hurry to get out and die, and there are a couple of misspellings, too. A few, I think. Not that it matters. He worked hard at that letter, very hard. And his plan to die went so well. I wonder how long he'd been preparing for his death? Had we chats and cosy cups of tea, and all the while in the back of his mind he was plotting on the best way to die?

Dear Mum, I don't want you to blame yourself for this. It's not your fault. If it's anyones fault, then you know who to blame, but not yourself. I've been so fed up lately, and I see no future in going on. What I've done I can't live with. There'll always be secrets hanging over my head. Whenever I look back I'll see my past, and I can't handle that. I feel all dirty inside, and I have to be honest and say that the thoughts of doing this, what I'm going to do, makes me happy. I won't have a past to trouble me because I'll have no future. I know you're going to be upset, and all, but its what I want to do. If I don't do something then I've got face knowing what I am – a pervert like Dad – I could turn out like him, couldn't I? I know I could. If I had a wish it would be for Dad to die, and I have often thought of doing it, shooting him the way he shoots dogs. I shoot them because they kill our sheep, he does because they kill the sheep, but also because it gives him pleasure. I have seen it in his eyes. Once, we walked along Chute's Path, by the derlict house, and a lame fox came out from the iron gate into Chute's old place. He was pathethic looking, half starved. Dad couldn't shoot him because he'd no cartridges. He asked had I any, and I said no because I knew what he was going to do. He went over and started to beat the fox with the buttstock. It whelped, and whined, and it took a lot of blows to quieten it. It lay there, its eyes open. The life going from them. It had yellow eyes. Its tongue fell from its mouth like the sole of a shoe had come off. He kicked it in the ribs and then walked away, saying fuck it, Adam, come on. I didn't follow him. He walked on, in through the furze, along a trail the horses take to the gallop, and I got to my knees and saw the fox was still breathing. I shot it. Its eyes took in mine, and then the life left them, and I got to thinking that at least it knows

no more pain. I envied him, I really envied him, Mum. The Path went silent, no birds sang, the skies seemed to disapprove. I caught up Dad in a clearing where he pissed against the furze, and had begun to button up his fly. He snorted and spat flem on to the grass, rubbing the sole of his boot on it. Then with his finger and thumb he took small tufts of fox hair from the buttstock and threw them away. If I had another cartridge I would have shot him that day. He boxed me because I'd lied to him about having no cartridges. I know this is going to be very hard on you, Mum, but please, please, this is my life, and I don't want to go on with it. It's just another way of dying. That's all. I'm just going sooner because I don't like the scenery, and I don't feel bad about it. I don't. I do love you, Mum, please explain to the others. It has taken me so long to pen this letter, to get it right, and in the end I could only find a red biro to go over it for the final time. I wouldn't know what to say to the others. I feel so dirty in myself, and the dirty way I feel is from Dad touching me, and it's a dirt that can't be washed away. Ever. And worse, Mum, the dirt spreads and spreads like some wild disease. I am Dad, a younger version of him, and you mightn't think that, and I would never want you think that, but I look like him, and I have his mark on me, and I could never stand you to look at me the way you look at him.
You might tell them I'm sorry. I'm sorry, Mum.
Don't think bad of me. Don't.
Adam.

Adam, if only I'd known, I could have said there is a way back, a way out. It mightn't be easy but there's a way. You were young enough to do a lot of good with your life.

The page riffles between Kay's thumb and forefinger. Kay sighs. 'It seems poor Adam blamed himself for Mike's actions.'

A pause.

'Need a fag,' she says. She zips her lighter and sets a flame to the corner of the page.

'Kay!'

Rushing over I snatch for the letter, but Kay is quick for her size and she brushes me away with one hand, the other going high, the flame brighter and redder.

'You don't need it … you don't.…'

She's a rock on her feet, pushing me away. I catch the smell of sweat from her armpits, catch the smell of burning paper and watch Adam's words go up in smoke and float about as black filament remains. I watch her, and when she throws the corpse of the letter into the fireplace, I slap her across the face. Her cheeks quiver.

'Kay – you'd no fucking right to do that, you bitch!'

Her lips tremble. I want to kill her. My son's last thoughts and words on this earth, and she had taken them away.

She grabs my shoulders and shakes me and God, how her eyes burn. 'You don't need it to live – there's nothing special about that letter. Nothing. The child was sick, he wasn't thinking straight. Are you listening to me? Are you?'

Her hands fall away. Like a pair of slates from a roof. Her eyes are like misted windows.

'Get out,' I say, shaking with rage.

Kay sways on her toes, panting. 'You've got the others to think about – Adam's gone.'

'You shouldn't have done that, Kay.'

'Well, I did … I promised myself I would.'

She points to the mantelpiece. 'There – see those photographs you have of Adam?'

Adam – his first day at school, his First Communion, with his friends. In the drawers his early school books, their scriggly scraggly scrawl, his Bs done back to front, his name, his first declarations, in ink, of who he was.

'That's how you should remember Adam. His letter wasn't a gospel of his life.'

'No – just his death – just go, Kay, go on – get out.'

Kay stares hard at me, then turns and leaves the room. Moments later, I hear the front door open and close. I'm vaguely aware of a small racket going on in the hall, maybe the kitchen. The sitting room door opens. Victor looks in, his nose twitching the air, catching the scent of his brother's burnt words. He says they are home, to come into the kitchen. His face is flushed. He says they have a surprise. I muster the bits and scraps of myself as best as I can, and follow him. They wait for me to speak. I can't. Frank wants to know what has sent Kay away in such a hurry. I say nothing, just gape at the straw basket beside the range in the kitchen. Pups!

'Tom gave them to the boys.'

'Tom can take them back.'

'Ah Mum,' Morris says.

Victor glares at me. I don't think he cares whether the dogs come or go.

'Morris – who's going to feed them, and clean up after them?'

'We will – or I will, by myself.'

'Just make sure you do, Mister, or they're out.'

I agreed because of the rats. But the pups are no bigger than the rats, and I suspect that if the rats don't eat them, the pups will grow to be rats. I'm not thinking straight at all. My stomach is in bits and my ulcer is acting up and I am out of Tagamet. My mouth ulcers are acting up too. I've had them a long time. God, I feel so down in myself. Kay, you shouldn't have done it.

Frank declines the offer of tea, says he's to make it back to the barracks to let a guy off duty. He mentions Fancy Lad on the doorstep and for a few moments I don't know what he is on about. Blank. Mind's a desert. Ah, the horse. Dogs and horses. I've just watched my son's suicide letter being burned in front of my eyes, by a woman I thought was my friend, and Frank wants to talk dogs and horses to me.

'He's good, Milly, really good … he'll win a race.'

I don't care. Silence tells Frank. He waits a few seconds for a response, then shaking his head he walks slowly to his jeep. Victor! Suddenly I have this feeling that of all the kids, the one to watch is Victor. The one whose broken wing mightn't heal. The one who speaks to me as though he hates my every living fibre, who gave me a horrible look when I asked him to leave out the key to Adam's room. I only wanted to clean out his room. I'd no intentions of prying; what on earth could he have in there?

I can't understand why he moved into Adam's room. Where's the attraction for him in it? What is going through his mind? I feel awful in myself.

Doors all round me lead to problems. Sometimes I wonder if they're all doors leading to a cancer like Julie's and Mum's.

The tests done on me and the girls came back negative. I didn't have to bring Karen or Gina with me, but I did, just to impress upon them that the females in our line are prone to getting breast cancer and they should get themselves screened every year at least. I'm more afraid of dying now than I ever was. Before, it was something that was down the road a bit, unless I got unlucky. Now, I've buried a younger sister, and a son. Gone before me and it doesn't seem fair. And it isn't fair. And sometimes my blood boils.

There's Julie who fought to live and Adam who fought to die. Pray harder for him? I have not managed to pray for him at all.

I mean pray, really pray. Pray for what? To whom? God? If God is almighty then why does he allow so much suffering in the world, why did he allow my son to wrap a rope around his neck? Why? Doesn't He feel for us – it's so very hard to imagine a God Almighty just standing by and letting a young fella kill himself. Questions, questions, and more fucking questions. *If You are there, will You help me, my family – stop your arseing about, and just fucking help.* It's the closest I can come to praying.

In the bathroom I see his empty space where his toothbrush used to be, ragged bristles made so by the tracks on his teeth, removed a month before he died. I'd been meaning to buy him a new toothbrush, and had the day before he hung himself. It's unopened in my handbag. It stares at me.

Jesus Chris Superstar! I went to see that local musical society presentation with Julie. The lights darkened and the spotlight came on Judas. And a thick rope. Julie hoped there were no people whose sons had killed themselves in that fashion in the audience. I don't believe there was then. At that point.

The days the boys were away seemed like forever. When they arrived in Frank gave me a slight shake of his head. The lads hadn't opened up.

A pair of terriers. Black and white, that Frank said wouldn't grow too big but would be faithful and loyal. When I asked if dogs killed themselves he looked at me and frowned. What I'd meant to say was that if either of the pups died, it'd just be another calamity that we didn't need right now. A risk. But Frank's eyes suggested that I was showing cracks.

'And once they're old enough – they've to stay in the stables. Not inside.' I say that harder than I intended.

Morris sighs, and says, 'Yeah, okay,' just to keep me off his back.

God help us. Where are we going? What's to become of us all?

Pat drops round later on that evening, after saying funeral prayers in Suncroft for a Mrs Touhy who died at home from a heart attack. I sit out front, where I never see any rats, and watch the sun setting out a cape of reds and ambers on the hills. I sit on a plastic garden chair and under a blue parasol Mike stole from the Curragh Racecourse. Mike has no conscience about robbing things. He changes price tags on stuff in shops, buying things at a lower price. (They've barcodes now, so he is cured of that. It's a pity his mickey and his hands aren't barcoded.) I call Gina and ask her to stick on the kettle. Pat sits opposite on the seat with the cracked plastic, the one that pinches your arse if you move a certain way.

'I heard,' he says.

'Some bitch, isn't she?'

He looks away, his hand a peak above his glasses. He resembles a card-dealer. He wears a blue woollen poloneck with a broken neck zip, revealing a yellow T-shirt and a gold crucifix and chain. His stepmother bought the crucifix for him in the Holy Land. It has smaller satellite crosses at each corner and a red opal fixed in the main cross. He says she bought it in Akko, a Jerusalem crucifix, very expensive. It's a nice way to make up after the years of coolness between them.

'What happened between you and your step–?'

He loosens a sigh and then says, 'She used to beat Dad. I mean she used to give him hidings. Mark him. I used to watch her through the stair rods – shout, scream, punch and scratch his face – she scared the hell out of us. When I think about – anyway, all in the past. I try to leave it there.'

He looks at his hands, as though sometimes he expects to see the marks of the Cross there. 'I've heard from Mike.'

I knew he would, that it'd only be a matter of time. 'You have?'

Pat nods, shows polished teeth on his lower lip.

'No, Pat ... I can't, not yet. Don't ask.'

Gina brings the tea. Pat asks her how she is going. Gina says she is going fine.

She leaves and returns with a jug of milk and a plate of chocolate biscuits. Pat takes off his glasses and rubs his eyes. I pour the tea. He likes his black with two sugars. Strong.

'He's selling the farm and has a buyer who wants the house as well. It'll be enough for you to afford a move away, Milly.'

'Where's he staying?'

Pat crosses his legs, smacks lips that have suddenly gone dry. 'Hotel Keadeen.'

Newbridge, about five miles away. Only five miles.

'He needs to get some things out … mainly from the shed, his tools and things. He knows you've got rid of everything else.'

'I can't believe you're on talking terms with that scum.'

His eyebrows climb. 'Neither can I.' His fingers light on his crucifix. 'But in my job we have to talk with them all. All, Milly. He rang and we had a chat. I didn't discuss Adam, or anything else with him, apart from the possible sale of the house, the return of his horses.'

'You'll be seeing him again?'

'Yes, and I think you should perhaps.…'

'I won't. No.'

I tell him that I'm considering reporting the matter to the guards. I would have done so ages ago but Gina asked me not to. She wants revenge and yet she doesn't want to go through the channels, to set the wheels in motion. In time, she says, she might, but she couldn't face court, not now, or him, not now.

Pat nods and spreads his hands. 'So, it's down the road a bit. I hope she finds the strength someday to do the right thing, to see him put away. It's what he deserves.'

'It's not the least thing he deserves.'

Pat sips at his tea, winces, and says, 'Your chair's cracked.'

We laugh. He has so much arse the chair must have taken a good bite. When we stop laughing I say, 'Yeah, I'll meet with him, but only if you're about and in the hotel lounge, so he can't start his antics.'

'Fine. I'll stay close.'

After a chat about general things, he asks about Kay. I tell him he is pushing things. Then I ask him to tell Mike that Annie keeps ringing me. She is looking for her husband's whereabouts. I don't think she believes me when I tell her that Mike is gone too. That I don't know where Ned is. The next time she calls I'm going to tell her to piss off and leave me alone. Pat says he'll talk with her. Just give her his number if she calls again. His tolerance of people makes me feel guilty.

I don't like Annie. She's a snobby bitch. She has a long, sharp nose with a birthmark right on its tip. A blemish I like, because it makes her look a little less than beautiful.

Still, she is married to Mike's brother and the two of us might be sharing similar pain, so I told her I would pass on word to Mike. Done through Pat. She didn't offer her condolences and I wondered why not, and what sort of a yoke would fail to do that? I hadn't noticed her at the funeral, or read a Mass card from her. Mike doesn't get on with Ned, and had never mentioned Annie. Not once. She's just the 'one' or the 'English yoke'.

Pat makes his excuses and says he'll give me a call. He adds that I might make enough to build a house on that site he gave me. It takes a moment for the memory to fire. I thought he was just saying it when he told me he had a site for me outside Limerick, but it's true. I forgot. A pity I can't forget the bad things as easily.

8

Morris

October

Karen screams when she walks into the dog piss on the lino. All the newspapers I put down, and the little fuckers had to wet the one spot of lino I missed. I should have left down the Page 3 girl but at the time I didn't think it looked right – not with the diddy problems in the house. Mum's funny when it comes to her breasts. I wish she didn't feel them in front of me. She doesn't even know she's doing it. She'd be miles away. Burying Julie and Adam all over, worrying about us. Thank God she keeps her hands above her jumper; I wouldn't know where to put myself if she forgot herself entirely.

'Those little fuckers,' Mum says, looking at the pups, who look back at her with big brown eyes, and then all our eyes meet at the yellow piss-ponds. A pup yips. He has to be Victor's, the brazen one, Mum adds. Uncle Frank got us the pups to make up for a miserable four days. It rained every day and we stayed in some creepy lad's creepy home the first night and in hotels afterwards. He and Victor didn't get along.

Uncle Frank's got a short fuse and Victor kept baiting him, from sticking a cigarette in his mouth to asking Frank if he were in the IRA. Frank looked at his coffee, then at the old Canadian ladies sitting behind us in the cafe, before eyeing up Victor, hard.

'Are you looking for a root up the hole?'

'Only asking.'

'I'm a soldier, not a terrorist.'

'Are you a deaf soldier, or an I-can-hear-when-I-want-to-sort-of-one?'

Victor knows how to get on peoples' nerves. Frank is half deaf in one ear and is suing the Minister of Defence for not providing him with proper hearing protection. Dad used to say Frank was a crook and soldiers shouldn't be allowed to sue. Mam said Dad was raging because he wasn't in the army to sue – just because you can't see the damage in a person doesn't mean it isn't there, she said to him – like some people with disturbed minds – you have to live with them to know. I got the feeling Mum was cutting at Dad about the disturbed minds bit. He just shot her a dirty look – a thousand *fuck offs* in his eyes.

Frank took a large sip of coffee, wiped his lips, looked at Victor, and shook his head.

'What?' Victor said. 'What's your problem?'

'Why are you saying things to bug me?'

'I'm not.'

'So, you're telling me your brain has lost control of your tongue?'

Victor nodded, put more ketchup on his burger and slugged at his cola. Belched. His mouth swollen with beef and bun, he licked some juice from his lip. Frank snatched the burger from his hand, slapped it on the plate, stabbed a finger in his chest. His eyes watered. He didn't know how to handle Victor. That came across loud and clear. Uncle Frank shouldn't be saying anything to Victor, should just watch and wonder, like the rest of us, about the stranger in Victor's body.

Victor realised he'd better cool things before Uncle Frank hit him a few slaps on the back of the head. Tell you the truth – I think Victor needs a few slaps on the back of his head. He's not the twin brother I knew. He doesn't even bother to read *Robinson Crusoe* any more. He left the book in my room. I killed a spider with it last week. As the book landed I wondered if the shock had knocked its eight legs from its body. Sick. But I was wondering, before the spider came on the scene, if Adam had any real notion what would happen to him once he jumped from the tree.

Did he have any idea what he'd look like lying in his coffin, his shirt collar buttoned to the last, to hide the rope burns? Or was getting out the main thing on his mind? Never mind the price, was living with us so bad? I bet if he knew how we all felt about him, he wouldn't have killed himself. I bet if he could have seen into the future and how much we're hurting, he wouldn't have jumped.

Frank's eyes lasered the bill and he capped the saucer with some notes. 'Out, you, ahead of me,' he barked to Victor.

Victor's eyes moistened, then hardened. He got up, dug a coin from his pocket and left it as a tip, and strolled out in front of Frank. That's the sort of time we had, Frank wishing Victor was ten years older so he could bruise his hole with a kick.

Victor called his pup 'R.I.P.' but pronounces it as 'Rip,' so as not to bug Mum. He's a little afraid of Mum. I called my dog Dono. I was going to call him Bono but I think Dono sounds better.

Mum said, 'Get them out into the stables ... I'm not having this, piss everywhere, except where it should be.'

So I made them up a nice straw bed in the box the grey horse used to stay in. Victor said I should drown them, that they're only a bloody nuisance. He's right, they are a bit of a nuisance, but so are lots of people, and we don't get rid of them for being nuisances.

Though when I think about it, maybe they kill themselves for us. I put a flea collar on Dono before settling him down for the night. I had bought one for

Rip as well, but Victor wouldn't let me put it on him. He said Rip was his dog and nothing goes around his neck without his say so. And he wasn't giving his say so.

'Don't you know what the fucking collar looks like, you moron? A noose, that's what,' he said.

I said nothing.

This night I look at Mum and decide to ask if the dogs can stay inside. Mum doesn't listen when I tell her that the pups will cry all night long in the stables. They won't like the dark and will go crazy when the rats come in to look at them. But she says, 'Outside with them,' in her most determined voice, and I don't answer her back, partly because I don't want to argue with her and partly because Victor is annoying me. When I get mad inside at people I go quiet. I think if more people did that there wouldn't be half as many arguments. I'm sure if Victor had spoken up Mum would have given the pups a last chance. It seems to me she'll do anything for Victor to keep him from becoming another Adam.

Victor used to be so kind to animals and insects. The old Victor would have given out to me for killing the spider, for instance. I think Adam's death has driven him up the wall.

Back in the kitchen, he's chatting with Karen. He seldom passes himself with Gina. As for the baby – he knows not to crawl anywhere near his … what? Are we Eric's brothers or what? His uncles?

Gotta figure that out, sometime. Daddy's daughter had a baby son by him + Daddy's wife had three sons and two daughters by him = ? Now, where does Gina figure in the equation? Daughter + son by Dad = Sister Mother. Yes. That's it. Gina is Eric's 'Sismum'.

One out of two isn't bad. Mum leaves the kitchen, saying she is going to have a lie-down. Lately, she's lying down a lot. Victor says if she hadn't been all the time lying down Adam would be alive now. That didn't make sense to me at all. But it makes perfect sense to him. Unlike the old Victor, he doesn't take the trouble to explain what I can't understand.

'Well, tell us, Karen ... how are things?' Victor says.

Karen's got a clear oval face. She's wearing a red ribbon and I've noticed her breasts have gotten bigger, which must concern her a lot. She looks at Gina when she answers Victor, 'Tell you about what things?'

Victor's eyes burn but he pushes a smile to his lips. 'Ah, come on ... about what happened between Mum and Kay.'

'I don't know.'

'What do you mean, you don't fucking know?'

Gina snaps, 'Listen here, you back off and leave Karen alone – if you must know, Kay burned Adam's letter, Mum told me, right, so just leave us alone.'

'What! She'd no fucking right to do that, at all.'

Gina puts the baby in his playpen. He whinges a little. Standing close to Victor, her fingers curling up into fists, she snarls at him, 'I'm sick of you – first you fight over seeing the counsellor....'

'What about him, what would I have to say to that fucking oul lad?'

Gina's features cloud. 'Tell him what you think about Adam killing himself.'

Hard to believe these two used to think the world of each other. Spitting venom.

Victor pulls his eyes from Gina's. 'Like would he ask about you screwing your daddy?'

Bang! One thing you don't do is to leave a Chef sauce bottle on the table when you're going to cut the arse off a woman. Victor doesn't know what hit him. His head lolls, blood drips from above his eyebrow. Karen's shriek frightens Eric into crying and Mum dashes from her room, in time to hear Gina say, 'Let that be a fucking lesson to you.'

Mum shouts, 'Call a doctor!' Victor's four stitches. Gina's sly smile. Karen, like me, keeping out of the way. Me seeing to the pups, pups that whinge to be let back in the house, where the bit of heat and comfort is. But you wouldn't bring a cockroach into our house with this atmosphere. It would turn over dead on its shell. So, I stay in the shed and break up a Mars bar among us. I stare out at the rain, watching the rainwater barrel by the back door fill to overflowing. The barrel is left handy because Mum likes to wash her and the girls' hair in rainwater, and for the dry toilet in the shed which Dad used because he could spend a long time in there without being bothered. Victor said he often saw Dad carrying two buckets of water to the shed, and that he must be trying to flush himself away but that he'd need a reservoir of water to do that. Victor got mad at me because he had to explain 'reservoir'.

Mum calls me in for tea. Victor stays in his room. He won't come out. It reminds me of Dad calling Adam the morning the sheep were killed. The way Adam didn't answer. The way we just put it down to Adam being in one of his moods. None of us knowing that this mood was the worst he was ever in, or would ever get in, again.

Gina's eyes are puffed up from crying. Eric creeps all over the place, on the rug in front of the fire, looking for ornaments to break or chew on. I suppose I'm lucky to cop it first, before Mum or Eric. A roll of dogshit lying under the sofa. God. The eyes in my stomach get sick at the sight of the sausages on my plate. Gina and Karen munching away. How the fuck am I going to get it out without them noticing? I hate dogshit.

Sometimes, when the blades of the mower chop up dogshit, the smell makes my stomach act up. Eric's heading that way. Curious brat. Probably thinks the shit is a chocolate sweet. I go over and pick him up. Everyone looks at me. I feel their eyes. I realise it's the first time I've touched Eric. He's got the tiniest little ribs.

He whinges like they do when they don't get their own way.

'Put him down, Morris,' Mum says, cross over us not getting her lie-down.

'He....'

'Put him down. I can't take his squealing.'

So, I do, but he isn't interested in going back to investigate the doggie matter; he wants Mum to hold him and makes his way to her chair.

She lifts him up and accuses him of smelling of pooh. She checks under his diaper and finds zilch. I sweat on this. If Mum sees the dogshit she'll freak.

'Must have blown, you dirty little man,' she says.

Just like his father I go to say, but my tongue guillotines my words. Lucky me.

I slip out of bed that night and clean up the shit. I feel sick for about an hour afterwards. And then I throw up everywhere. All over the place. But a smell of dogshit didn't cause my vomiting. Sheer worry and fear did the trick. I worry about a few things. Victor, he's sick, I know that. His eyes are dead in his head and he mumbles a lot. And Victor never used to mumble, unless he was calling Dad a name and didn't want him to hear. Now he sleepwalks or he pretends he's sleepwalking.

Gina isn't well either, but she's tough. Her nerves are just a bit loose, that's all. And she should be sicker than Victor. I mean, Dad touched her and did things with her, and she had a baby from him. I mean, no one could blame her if her mind packed up and left her body behind. Like Mrs Travis's did.

Mum's annoyed that none of her friends come over to visit. None of our friends ever appear on the doorstep. You would think we have the plague. Victor said there is one big fucking X on our front door, one only us lot can't see. Dildo doesn't drop round any more to swap his comics.

He was the guy who I expected to see at the front door on the day Father Toner came to tell us Adam was dead. I mean I wished so hard for him to be the guy, but wishing is like dreaming. I knew what Father Toner was going to say before he himself did.

Even Kay doesn't come around any more. She calls Mum a few times but Mum says to say she isn't in. She used to say it out loud so Kay could hear. Kay shouldn't have burned Victor's letter. Mum wasn't ready for that to happen and I've never seen her so bitter. I guess she feels like Jesus did when Judas betrayed Him, or General Custer did when he saw loads more Indians instead of the few he expected, or the people in this country with all these tribunals over people getting money they shouldn't have been getting, because it was wrong and that. I know Kay thinks she did right, but the way Mum looks at it she's been betrayed by just about everyone close to her.

There's Julie – God betrayed Mum there – He did, I think. Letting Gran and Julie die from the same disease. There's Victor – he hates Mum, every inch of her, and the rest of us. There's Dad – and he's still betraying her. Frank – he shouldn't have got those

dogs. Adam – the biggest traitor of us all. Queenie Travis – who sent Mum a Mass Card for Adam and a week later a letter telling Mum to stop Adam from robbing her orchard. Mum cried, not at what the letter said, but over Adam, wishing he were here to rob orchards, and for Queenie, who's madder than we all thought.

Friends and neighbours assorted – who gave up calling round.

I'll probably see Dildo on Monday, when I go back to school. I know what they're all thinking, but Mum is right – they have no right to look at us the way they do. We're not freaks. We're not freaks at all. Besides, Dad might be Eric's father, but at least Gina knows who the daddy is. There are a lot of women in town who couldn't, hand on heart, say which of their kids is by their legal daddy. And that's a fact. I know from listening to Aunt Julie, who told Mum all the stuff that went on in town. There's a thing about me that makes people forget I'm around and they just yap on a dozen words to the penny.

I might look stupid but I haven't got the wind tunnel people think I have between my ears. I knew what Aunt Julie meant when she said, 'And you know who from – number-one-nine-one two is sleeping with you know who from the Big Dong, where dogs howl.'

Easy peasy. Whoever lived in number 1912 was doing a line with a priest. Big Dong's the church bell,

and the dogs howl when it's rung. No daw, me. Telling Aunt Julie was my worst mistake. She said what her brother said to Victor, about getting a root up the hole.

Mum comes from one violent family.

I saw Mrs Travis the other morning, on our way to Westport. She's lost weight. Her hair has gone completely grey and her glass eye, the eye that never shuts, looked me up and down as though it were cursing me. In my nightmares I see her standing at the end of my bed, bouncing her eyeball on her palm. Saying something I can't hear, the wind tossing her words and her hair. The nightmares are bad, but at least you wake up from them, and say, 'Thank God, it's only a dream,' but I couldn't say that when I was scooping the dogshit up from the kitchen.

I was on bended knee, careful not to break the skin of the shit, so the smell wouldn't mess me up, and then I heard something behind me. A fall of foot. Adam. Or so I thought. I screamed but nothing came out. It was Victor wearing Adam's favourite tracksuit. And I thought all Adam's clothes had been burnt or given to the Sue Ryder shop in Newbridge. He opened the back door and walked out. I followed him as far as the door, but I lost sight of him when he went beyond the reach of our security light. I went in for Mum.

It drizzled, and blinded by the darkness, we walked in and out of puddles. My arms got goosepimples and puddle water ran over the rims of my slippers, soaking my feet. I wondered if rats pissed in the puddles – you can die from touching rat piss – if you don't wash your hands and you eat some food, you could be dead within a few hours. I told myself that I didn't eat with my feet so I should be okay.

'Victor!' I shouted, wondering if I should have called 'Adam' instead.

Mum shushed me, saying you don't waken the sleepwalking. We didn't know where he had got to. I thought that he had gone to the locked shed, because it was in the dark and I couldn't see a thing beyond that wall of darkness. The yard was huge and there were old sheds with tin roofs, where Grandad used to keep pigs. We don't go into them any more because they're full of cobwebs and no doubt rats, pucks of them.

'Mum….'

I thought we should check the stables.

I studied Mum through the raindrops. Grey going greyer, a coat over her shoulders. The light rain was turning to heavy.

Reaching the stable door, I pulled it open; the hinge squeaked, the other was broken so it scraped the ground – there was a squeak and scrape and rustle from something in the hay, darting by us, Mum's shrill scream hitting the air. She stepped back. The stable was dark and I felt as though my insides were melting. Dad had got electricity in the stables. He wanted to get in infra-red lights because they were warmer and easier on the horses' eyes if left on all night. In the end he never got to buying the bulbs. That's the sort he is, he never finishes anything he starts.

Us

'Victor, are you in there? It's me, Morris,' I said, like he had to be told it was me, though it made sense to tell him; hadn't he become a stranger?

Silence, except for the rain hitting the tin roof, the trees shivering and the sound of a train way off in the distance beyond the fox covert and the golf club.

'Victor?' I knew he was somewhere close but he kept to the shadows.

I dropped to my hunkers and went unsteady, my fingers falling on something wet. I made a mental note to wash my hands. Dono emerged. Dono licked at my toes and wagged his tail. Rip was probably asleep. It was then I noticed that I had dogshit on my fingertips. The smell. Mum tugged at my arm. I knew it was her because I smelled her perfume. I put Dono back in the stable and after the squeak of hinge bolted the door. I don't like locking up animals – it's not right. I wish there were something I could do about the rats; the pups would whimper when they saw them. It could have been a funny night. Something to tease Victor over.

He ended up back in bed with muddied feet. Mum shook her head and bit her lip to stop a tear from falling. Victor wearing Adam's tracksuit. It could have been a funny night but it wasn't.

Drying off in the bathroom, I filled the wash basin and put in some Dettol. I spent five minutes washing my hands and then I put on the fresh T-shirt and boxers I'd taken from the hot press and slipped across to my room, sliding the bolt across behind me and flicking the switch. My bed was in shite, all mucked up, and the window was wide open.

We never leave the windows wide open, because of the rats. I closed the window and fetched Mum. She changed the sheets while I looked everywhere for a sign of a rat. She said I could keep Dono indoors with me from now on, though I knew she didn't mean it.

Victor is pale in the morning, not touching his Sugar Puffs. The rain stopped but not for long I felt, just taking a rest in the overcast skies before starting up again, probably when it was the most inconvenient time for us; the bay window was crowded with raindrops, Heaven's Tears, Mum calls them.

I hear Frank's jeep coming round the back, its engine cutting out with a familiar splutter, and Frank, seconds later, shouting out loud, 'Lord Jesus Christ!' That brings Mum and me running. (The girls aren't up – and Eric is in his highchair.)

'What?' Mum says, alarm high-pitching her tone, drying her hands in the apron Julie brought her back from Costa de Titty, as Dad said, being funny and cruel at the same time, as only he can.

I expect to see a cluster of rats or something. I'm sure Mum thinks likewise.

His eyes drag ours to the rainwater barrel.

Mum's hands shoot to her face. Mine don't know what to do. I think my fingers curl in and out, looking for someplace to hide. Rip's tiny paws rest over the rim, his head just breaking the water, his ears bent over like someone has dampened them down.

Frank scoops him out and, dropping to his hunkers, examines the pup. A dark, wet rag, with fluffs of white on his paws, small marks that stand him apart from Dono. Brown eyes open. Another creature not believing he is dead.

We stand there. Shocked. Mum touches Frank's shoulder and then mine. She needs support. She feels awful heavy.

I go into the kitchen while Mum and Frank speak outside, after Frank buries Rip around the back of the stables where the tractor is kept and the rats play hide and go seek in the nettles and thistles. Gina is feeding Eric. She wears her pink dressing-gown. She's always losing its buckle and sometimes the gown opens and I can see her knickers and her long skinny legs, but Mum got on to her about it and now she wears pyjamas underneath, and so, this morning, I see nothing only little blue elephants on her pyjama top and a spot of egg-stain.

Victor says nothing. He munches on his cereal. He is eating them dry, from a bowl, with a teaspoon, a glass of milk in his hand. He doesn't query the fuss, shrugs when he hears of Rip's death. 'When you gotta go, you gotta go,' he says.

'He drowned, Victor.'

'Did he? I told him to watch out for the puddles.'

'You were sleepwalking last night.'

'I was, was I?' His eyes dive in at the corners.

He plays his forefinger along his stitches, and winces – I see the pleasure he takes in the pain – his eyes light up like neon signs, winking blue. He touches his stitches again and smiles. Scary. He's so fucking scary.

'Well, your sheets must have been muddy – you got in my bed and then Adam's – you muddied everywhere. Didn't you notice how muddy your sheets were, the dirt on your feet?'

He pushes his bowl away. 'What are you telling me – that I killed Rip, is that so, Mister? Let me tell you this – if I wanted to kill someone, I'd shoot him, not drown him. Right?'

His tone prompts Gina to hold baby Eric tightly to her chest and Mum to gather in the collar of her cardigan close to her throat. Karen bites the back of her hand. And Victor, looking through us, at a *Tom and Jerry* cartoon on TV, gives the strangest of small smiles.

Frank's in, washes his hands, says he would love a cup of ultra-strong tea. Pouring himself some tea, because no one had stirred to pour for him, he says to Victor, 'Are you okay, son?'

Bad choice of word – *son*. Typical of Frank.

'Yeah. Okay.'

'Do you want to come for a walk?'

Shake of head.

'Come into town?'

'No. I'm watching TV.'

'Do you know what happened to Rip?'

'He's dead. Morris told me.'

'Do you know how he died?'

'He drowned, didn't he – better than hanging himself I suppose, isn't it?' Victor scrunches up his face. For the first time, he looks at Frank, 'Did he hang himself?'

Frank doesn't ask any further questions. He is lost. No good for doing anything, unless it requires a root up the hole. And Victor looks as if a thousand of those wouldn't bother him.

Mum rings Kay. It makes me think how quickly we forgive things when we want to.

Victor has us all in a heap. One thing is for sure, Dono is sleeping with me tonight and my bedroom door will stay locked, in spite of Victor telling me there is no need, now that Dad isn't around.

A minute after Mum gets off the phone it rings. Mum freezes. Her hand makes a jerky movement towards the phone. 'Hello?' she snaps, looking at us as she lifts the phone. Some of her colouring returns. Mum sighs in relief. 'Sorry, Pat, sorry for being so short – I didn't expect you to ring so quickly – thanks – I'm so….'

Mum nods. 'No. Make it half-seven, you'll be there? Aha, okay, that's good – we're all a little stunned here, you know, you can guess.'

Mum and Gina had said they weren't going to report Dad; there were too many minuses. Media glare would be focused on Gina and Eric and Adam. With the rest of us getting sucked in. Better to make Dad pay through his nose, so we could go buy a house down the country, make up our own past and act like a normal family.

Mum nods, 'That's settled … no, don't come here, Pat, not yet … I'll see you this evening.'

Victor cuts in, 'Let him. Let Dad come home.'

Mum says goodbye and puts down the phone. She holds onto the phone for a few moments, gripping hard, like she did when she rang Julie's after she died, just to hear Julie's voice on her answering machine.

Mum runs her eyes over us, 'Step one in putting all this behind us.'

Victor nods and doesn't stop nodding. Not even when Kay walks in an hour later. She takes Mum out for a drive and for the first time I feel all alone. Karen stays in her room, listening to her music. Gina plays with Eric, and Victor sits in his room, talking to himself. I'm glad to see Tom come in.

He and Frank stay for a few minutes, they tell me to tell Mum the horse is entered in a race at Naas next Tuesday. I say I will and Frank says he'll bring me and Victor. It's something to look forward to, although with our luck the horse's legs will probably fall off before he reaches the starting line. I remember a horse belonging to Uncle Tom taking a heart attack after finishing second in a race. The chestnut shuddered all over and then died. Tom says she died almost as quickly as his marriage.

Us

I knock on Victor's room but get no answer, so I turn the brass knob and go in. My stomach ices over – he is sitting on the bed, looking at the wall, running a yellow dust-cloth over the shotgun on his lap. I see the cartridges in the barrel and watch him close the stock and point the gun at me.

'What's that feel like, Morris ... someone pointing a gun at you?'

'Not nice.'

On his feet, pointing the gun low, he says, 'I'm going to plug a few rats. Do you want to bring in your pup in case I get him by accident?'

'Yeah ... yeah, I better. Thanks for telling me, Vic.' I always call him Vic when I want something from him or to show my gratitude when he gives me something.

I fly into the kitchen and tell Gina to get herself and Eric into the room, that Victor is going shooting rats. She puts this stupid look on her face and doesn't move until I remind her that Victor is always calling her and Eric rats and then she moves like a Curragh gale.

I stay in my room, counting the reports, Dono going crazy each time there's a bang. There are ten shots. I reckon Victor has about twenty cartridges all told, maybe more. I try to think of a plan – how do I get that shotgun away from him?

BOOM!

Dono whimpers. I pick him up and lie down with him on the bed. He creeps towards my chin and settles on my chest. Then I move him because I realise if there is another pellet blast he might wet me. But there is no more.

Minutes later Victor knocks on my door and says, 'Morris … I got loads.'

I open the door to him. He has two black sacks in his left hand, the shotgun in the other, a smile on his face, a dance in his eyes. Blood, there is blood on his shoes, and small tears in one of the black sacks, a tear widening before my eyes, and a dead rat, its insides hanging out, plops onto the carpet. I feel like puking my guts up. Dono sniffs at the rat, his inch of tongue tipping it. I poke him in the arse with my toe and tell him to get the fuck away.

Victor stoops and picks the rat up and puts it back in the bag. Then he says, turning about, 'Maybe it's better if we count them outside.'

I look at the rat guts on the floor and tell Victor I'll follow him out. I clean up the mess and make the kitchen sink in time to heave up – baby carrots and chicken – Jeezus – I wash my sick and then I throw the rat mess into the bin outside and find that Victor has emptied the black bags inside. I don't know why he didn't bury the rats. Fuck. If Mum or the girls raised the lid of the bin – the screams – imagine? He is out of it. That's for sure. Totally. With the fairies. I get sick on top of the rats and then slam the bin lid shut, scaring Dono. He whimpers. I tell him to fuck off and that I am going to scrub out his fucking tongue with Dettol. Licking at rat guts.

'Victor!' I yell. I'm mad at him and afraid of him too. But right now my anger is sky-high, much stronger than my fear.

I spot him then, heading across the fields, the shotgun broken, a cigarette going to and from his mouth. He looks so much like Adam. Lots of me hope that like Adam he won't be coming back.

9

Frank

October skies are grey and full of the threat of rain. I am in the jeep outside my trailer, with the engine and my thoughts ticking over. A shelterbelt of pine shivers in the rising wind. I've just left Milly's place, dropping Tom in Kildare where he'd to meet with a horse owner in The Vatican pub. Tom's as sick at heart as I am, and he'll drink a couple of scotches to bolster himself against the *mundanities* of life, as he calls them. He can't take in what I've told him about young Victor and shakes his head in answer to his own thoughts.

When I saw the pup in the barrel I gulped to swallow vomit. It left a sourness in my throat. I mean, fuck, I still can't believe it. I thought of the Leb' and the dogs rotting under sun and sea-spray on the beaches of Tyre. I thought of the two Fijians lying dead on the side of a road, at a checkpoint, a week to going home, a week to smelling aviation fuel in Beirut Airport, a week to seeing their wives and kids.

And Adam, dangling from an apple-tree in Queenie Travis's orchard, his eyes gaping wide and lifeless. Unseeing. Cutting him down he vomited on me, and I screeched from the fright and disgust, and Tom and some others caught some of the foulness as well. We laid him on the ground, leaves under him, stars above him, and stood back.

Someone whispered an Act of Contrition in his ear, and another said a 'Hail Mary' out loud. No one joined in.

A tall guard with a long face said it was the way we cut him down; he said we should have held him from behind and then cut the rope, that way he wouldn't have spewed on us. He didn't know I was Adam's uncle. He spoke as though Adam were the latest in a long list of corpses he'd seen, and toe-tagged – '*Just routine, nowadays*,' he said.

I went back to Queenie's the next day. She was away in some neighbour's house, getting to grips with herself. After a couple of days she ended up in a home, going through a range of treatments to jigsaw her mind together. There's a small crack in the gable end of her cottage, running zig-zag from tip of the chimney to where the downpipe meets the shore. Queenie's place is in bad order. Entering the orchard, its surrounding wall broken in one place, probably the spot where it fell on Queenie when she chased the boys, the concrete the colour of bone, I took in the *scene*.

Yellow Scene of Crime tape cordoned off the tree and the patch where we rested Adam. Present only until the guards could check the scene during daylight hours, I was told. There was evidence of climbing, the long-faced guard said, and the stepping-off point was from a strong limb.

I wrapped up the tape and left it by the tree, coiled up like a yellow snake. The air smelt of dead apple. Suicide, the guard said. *What was his name? Richards?* Doesn't matter.

Rip. Jesus. He felt soft and soggy in my hands, and his brown eyes like cut glass appeared to be full of questions. I closed them. The blood ran from Morris's face.

And poor Milly's knees buckled. Victor – I know he killed Rip. I don't know whether Victor knows he did. He's going about with his eyes half-closed and the open half-glazed. He frightens the hell out of me. Milly's going to see Father Toner and Kay Walsh. I think she should get a doctor in to see young Victor. But Milly doesn't think for one moment that Victor killed Rip. I know by her. She hasn't got around to questioning who might have.

I didn't tell anyone, not even Tom, that Rip didn't drown. He was strangled. I saw the marks on his neck and found the blue string a couple of feet away, right at my jeep's door where it looked like it was left for me to find. Of course, it wasn't.

I get out of the car and climb the steps of the veranda, taking small comfort in the soft, familiar creak of the boards, and turn the key in the door. I take a beer from the fridge, and before its door closes I snatch two more and break for the sofa, setting the beers on the low coffee table, remoting the portable TV to life.

I need the beer in me and then I've some calls to make. Father Pat and Doc Fleming in Kildare, who all know Milly, who might have a look at Victor. I quit the army yesterday, pension earned and Fatima waiting for me in Beirut, something to look forward to: fine weather and a good woman. Perhaps out there I can get round to giving up the booze. I hate the way it owns me but love what it does for me.

Detta's a bitch. I hate her guts. When I admit to hating her I know I'm getting drunk. I miss Sam. Fuck Fred Tex anyway. A larger-than-life Dad for my boy. Fuck him for being so much better than me – for having steadier hands.

Queenie with the one eye. God love her. Why did Adam choose to die in her back garden, among her crab-apple trees? Why do what he did in the first place? Well, we know the answer to that. His father abused him – Mike, the fella I told Milly was a sound bloke. Jesus, I could never read a person right. I never see fault in anyone, blind to them until they do something glaringly wrong. No third eye.

I knew Queenie's husband, Bob. A prick with ears and nose. They came to live around here about thirty years ago. Queenie came without her eye, without her son, who'd been killed in the same car accident Queenie'd been involved in, a road pile-up on a frosty winter's morning. She showed my Mum the newspaper cutting. It made the front page news on the *Evening Press*. Bob drove too fast, she said. He was always driving too fast. He never listened to her, not to a word she said.

We got to know them because Bob delivered fuel in the Curragh Camp. He had a few plots of turf out by Monasterevin which he used to draw from, and some others he didn't own but which he drew from, in Allenwood, beyond the power station they demolished last year.

He was a quiet, gruff man with a bad stammer. Almost bald with a little sneer that came to his mouth every so often, like it decided to sneak up from his soul and give us a glimpse of the real man. He used to beat Queenie, regularly. I don't know how a woman puts up with that shit. I never hit a woman and by Christ I'm not saying it's easy to stay the hand, because it's not. I often felt like lashing out at Detta and I often felt that's exactly what she wanted me to do.

Queenie loves watching *Coronation Street* and *Glenroe*. If I want to get her to talk, all I've got to do is give out about one of the characters and she'll join in, agreeing with me, because one thing Queenie doesn't do is disagree with people.

Six green cans and another six in the fridge. Calls. Calls, later. This is good. I light a cigar. I love

Hamlet, the roll of its smoke in my mouth. Where was I ... Queenie, yeah, who took her revenge when Bob fell ill with cancer of the throat – or stomach? It doesn't matter, it went through him in the end. She mixed up his medicines or gave them to him later than he needed or asked for them. *Ricki Lake*. She watched *Ricki Lake* the night Adam killed himself. She loved the show, the rows between couples; wasn't it brilliant, she said, to know there's always someone worse off than you?

Queenie with the sore hands always an angry red, the whiskers on her receding chin, her tea-stained teeth, mirthful crinkles about her eyes, a mole on her cheek sprouting a lone hair. Dressed in blue kaftan, the long robe embroidered with silver thread, a garment my mother gave her, because wasn't she, Queenie, a distant relation, and her blood, no matter how diluted, was of our blood? I wonder if that's where we get the strain of madness ... Queenie?

Shush, don't tell anyone else, I tell myself.

The army didn't do a whole lot to keep me. I'm thirty-eight, with a drink problem, a claim against the Minister pending and have turned too contrary for them, I suppose.

Still, I've enjoyed my time there, most of it anyway. The future matters, not the past. I keep telling Milly that, but not bluntly; I tell her it's time to look forward, not back.

What am I going to do with myself in Lebanon? A deaf weapons instructor won't find many jobs waiting for him. Fatima says she'll find me part-time work in a hotel bar. I might take her up – at least I won't get homesick.

I helped Rafi, Fatima's brother, to dodge conscription by giving him a thousand dollars. He's married with two kids and living in a poor suburb of Beirut, not far from the Airport Road. Electricity wires criss-cross from roof to roof, making a canopy of cord above the road. The houses are drab and every second one seems to be a garage or butchers. I'd come up from Tibnin that morning to find Fatima consoling her younger brother. He's thin as a rake and a very nervous sort of person. He told me that he received his call-up papers for the Lebanese Army, and was to report in for his medical the day after tomorrow. He would be trained at Leb Army Headquarters in Yardze, a place I knew of, with its skyscraper monument of tanks and jeeps set in concrete. After that, because he's Christian, he'd see out his military service in South Lebanon, possibly up against the Israeli-backed Christian Militia. So we brought him to a doctor in Hamra Street looking for a medical excuse, but the first guy we went to shook his head and said he wasn't involved in that sort of thing. But after Fatima pleaded with him, he gave us a name. It fell from his tongue, like it was something gone sour.

This guy agreed for a thousand dollars to fix Rafi up. He made him chew gum for about an hour and then drop it onto his gloved hand. He stretched the gum to a very fine thinness and placed it along Rafi's left leg, X-raying then. The negative showed a fine crack along Rafi's leg, a typical result from a motorbike fall. He didnt do his military service. I wish money could have cured Adam's problems in the same way, that there'd been a way out for him and that I could have helped.

I must have fallen asleep. I wake to find the place in darkness, the trees tipping against the sides. I'm cold and sick in the stomach. Sky One's music show is on TV. Cher and her Shoop song. Jesus. A belch of stale beer.

Four a.m. and three beers in the fridge. I leave them there and go to the bedroom at the back and climb into bed, searching for sleep that doesn't come. Instead, I lie on my back and fight off the urge to piss.

The room is dark and silent, the silence broken by an occasional creak of springs from under the mobile.

Mike. He's in the country, staying not far from here. Somewhere nearby, Milly said, declining to tell me where exactly. She has good reason. I've every intention of seeing Mike and it'll be close to a river or on a motorway bridge, where he'll take a fall, or perhaps in a place in the bog where Bob once brought me to help him load his turf into hessian sacks and showed me a bog-hole that'd swallow a man good and proper, covering him with an unfathomable depth of mud. That's what I'd like to do, the dreamer me. Milly wouldn't be interested in knowing my ideas; in fact, she'd be angry. She said nothing, not even thanks, when I sorted him out before. Instead she smouldered and glanced away from me, as though I'd done something disgusting. What is it with her?

Perhaps she sees through me and knows I hit Mike because I need to hit someone because of my frustrations with life: my marriage break-up, my distant son, my booze addiction, the constant ringing noise in my ears that sometimes keeps me awake nights, which the specialist called tinnitus, which the army's legal eagles incline to believe is a figment of the imagination, or something trivial, and not necessarily caused by exposure to gunfire. I stood on the range over the years, training and instructing guys, correcting firers' faults: grip, stance, sight-picture, breathing, control. The smell of cordite strong on my clothes, its grey, dark shadow about my nostrils. A burnt powder smell and never again a strange one.

So Milly saw through me then. Mike wasn't hit for hitting her, that was only part of the reason. The dreamer in me wants Mike dead, but I know what dead is, what it looks like, what it smells like, and I don't like it. I think when you kill someone you don't know how much you've taken away from him – you can guess – but you don't know, and you don't know what's coming down on you and yours for murder; in this life or the next. But if that's the case, what happens people who murder themselves?

It comes to a point, maybe, when you realise that life isn't what you think it is and was never what you thought it was, that in the end what you did, said, doesn't count, because you were nothing before and you're on the way to going back to being nothing, and does it matter then, how you go or when you go, because you're going there anyway? I'm really fucking drunk.

I'd a row with Tom at Dublin Airport, after Adam's funeral.

'He got a good turnout,' I said.

'He did.'

'Little bollocks.'

'Shush, Frank....'

'Shush me hole, go to be fucked with your shush, Tom – he was a little bollocks for doing it. Did you see the state of Milly, for Christ's sake....'

'The young fella was sick, Frank, go easy on him.'

Tom touched my shoulder, then shook it, 'Go easy on him!'

I get out of bed and take a leak and then put on the water for coffee. My mouth is dry. There's a speck of a cold sore at the corner of my lips. A shiver inches up my back. The onset of a flu. I brew coffee, call Tom to say I won't be at Fancy Lad's final hard gallop and go back to bed. Flu … depression? Does it matter, what matters? Either way, I'm sick.

We call round for the boys first thing on Tuesday morning. They were supposed to start school yesterday but Milly gave them an extra week's holiday. Morris climbs in the back after Victor. Morris smiles hello; the other lad says nothing. I catch him in the rearview mirror. His eyes don't have that half-shut look. I had rung Milly and suggested the idea that she bring Victor to see Doc Fleming. She went quiet, as though she resented my intrusion. She said Pat and Kay had given her advice – the way she said it made me think she was telling me she'd received enough advice. Of course, I knew she blamed me for giving the lads the dogs. I shouldn't have, but then I thought they might have been a distraction. I told her getting the dogs was a bad call.

She said it was, and then she said she'd met with Mike, and I stopped her. I was thick with her about the dogs and said I didn't want to know. After a moment's silence she told me about the rats in the bin, the carpet she had to lift, and I asked her if she was really, really sure she didn't want Doc Fleming to see Victor. She hung up on me. Mike … she's going to see him. Milly always had a strong stomach.

Tom chats away and Morris chats back when Tom's mouth takes a break. He's all talk about Dono, how he is training him to shit and piss on newspaper and that he sometimes sits when told, and other times he doesn't, because he wants to play.

Victor is dark. He tells me his dad is staying in Hotel Keadeen. I know he says this for a purpose. Tom and me just swap glances.

Tom's trained four winners this year, which is good going from an eight-strong stable, two of whose number are crippled along with Mike's other horse, who's useless. The flat season is drawing to a close. Tom's horses are pushing on in years and he keeps them for the jumps during the winter. Fancy Lad is a sprinter and Tom says he's letting loose a lot of money on him. He's set to lay two grand at ten to one. I told him to put a thou' on for me and one for Milly. He nods and pockets my cheque. It is a small backend of season race meeting, with not many punters attending. The going is softish and some of the fields too large to make picking a winner any easier than picking the right Lotto numbers, but Fancy Lad is in a field of eight, the only grey, easy to spot.

I lead the horse to the pre-race stables and remove the bandages from his forelegs, catching the smell of iodine in my nostrils. He has developed sore shins but is fit enough to race. Tom has gone to check that his punters have turned up to place the bets and to get the silks he'd forgotten in the car.

'My da's here,' Victor says in a droning tone.

I look at Morris, who shrugs.

Morris needs braces. His eye-teeth are growing out of place. Victor probably needs them as well, but he never opens his lips enough for me to see.

'You're sure, Victor?' I say.

'Wouldn't I know him a mile away? He's wearing a blue suit.'

'You're sure?'

'Yeah, he's here to take back his horse.'

'Is that so?'

'I heard Mum telling Kay.'

Morris's eyes are all over the place. I look about but don't spot Mike. Tom is making his way over, the silks draped across his forearm. I put the reins and saddle on Fancy Lad, fit his noseband and blinkers. Tom will check everything after me, not because he doubts my work, but because that's the way he is, he believes no one can do anything better than himself.

'Did you see Mike on your travels?' I say.

'No.'

I take in Victor. Perhaps he is seeing Mike's face in everything. He looks tense and drawn, eyebrows furrowed. Jesus – Mike – look at the effect your presence is having on your lad. Fucking shite it is.

The horses circle the Parade Ring, making a clatter on the gravel walkabout. The jockey on board Fancy Lad sits, quietly confident. He is three wins short of the leader in the Jockey Championship for most wins. I pray hard he'll be two after the next twenty minutes.

I bring the boys up onto the grandstand. Through the binoculars I see the horses being fed into the starting stalls by green-helmeted handlers, a chestnut with the sweat foaming up shies away, causing a delay.

'The white flag is raised – they're off!'

'Where is he, where is he?' Morris says, his voice rising.

'Middle of the field, on the outside, he's the only grey, Morris.'

I observe the horses, their flaring nostrils, their hooves cutting the turf into thick clods, specking the air with them. The jockey nudges Fancy Lad alongside the sweaty chestnut at the final furlong pole. Things look promising. Coasting, riding our lad hands and heels. And then, a bay horse bolts from nowhere and pins Fancy Lad on the line. I've seen enough photo finishes to know we are going to hear the wrong result. Shit.

Morris says, 'Fuck it,' under his breath.

Victor says, 'Fuck him,' above his breath.

I reproach neither – how can I? – when sometimes the bad language slides off my own throat. Lead by example is right.

I say we are hard done by but that's how it goes. We make a move to meet Tom. He stands outside the Parade Ring, looking grim as a Curragh sky on a wet day. He should have been inside, smiling at the jockey when he dismounted but bollocking him out because of the poor ride he gave our horse.

'What's up, Tom?'

'The owner showed up.'

I look past his shoulder. He puts a hand against my chest, 'Don't Frank … not here.'

Mike stands like a lord inside the compound, clapping hands. The bastard. I look at the two boys and my blood boils. My mouth begs for a drink. I push Tom aside and storm for Mike. Suddenly I want to live out my dream.

He sees me coming. Holding Fancy Lad's bridle, the jockey by his side, busying himself with uncinching the saddle to try and hide his look of guilt and to keep his eyes from meeting mine.

'You've a fucking nerve coming in here,' I say.

'It's my horse, why wouldn't I be here? Second place prize isn't to be sniffed at, and his value has gone up. He'll fetch a good price.'

The jockey mumbles an excuse and leaves, tapping his crop against his thigh.

'I gave you a warning.'

'Not in front of witnesses, Frank, the law is on my side.'

'It won't be when the cops get an earful of what Gina has to say.'

'She won't go to the police, Frank … I know that. Milly does too. You're about the only one who doesn't. Get wise.'

I hit him hard. Maybe I break his jaw because I hear it crack. He falls backwards. I stand over him, and say, 'That's for Adam.'

Not for me, not even a little of it. Then I leave him there and walk from the parade ring. Fuck him. Tom walks away with the boys, and stops near a stall to buy fruit and chocolates from Enid the Mayo Woman. I'm panting hard and feeling jumpy. I don't feel a pinch of satisfaction. I know then, that no matter how much and how often I burst Mike, it isn't going to improve matters one teeny fucking bit. I can't burst my way to the past and make everything all right.

Lost our money, lost our horse, lost my temper and threw a fist. Tom gives me a litany on the way home. The boys are silent. Like me, I bet they're thinking it would be great to be a winner in this life, just once, just fucking once, to know how it feels.

10
Milly

October

The horse lost. They all made excuses. Frank said the jockey dropped his hands and the winner stole by him. Tom nodded and then shook his head, saying the horse would have won with Homer Simpson on board, with anyone other than the clown he saddled up. Morris said at least Fancy Lad proved he could run, if not quickly enough, and Victor said he saw his dad, and perhaps the horse did too, and the sight of him drove the horse back a yard. A notion to ponder.

We sit in the kitchen drinking tea. It pours rain and there is no sign of a let-up.

I know Frank and Tom have gambled away a lot of money. Tom's pale and when he worries he bites his nails. He tries not to in my presence but I still read his worry. Frank is distant, rubbing his hand, trying to hide his scraped knuckles from me.

'You were fighting,' I say.

He looks at me and then drops his gaze to his cigarette on the pink ashtray he brought me back from Lebanon.

'He bursted Dad,' Victor says in a voice that suggests Frank should receive a medal.

'You can't keep your hands to yourself, can you? Can you?'

'He asked for it.'

'And you obliged him. When are you going to stop wading into battle on my behalf? What is it with men that they can't keep their fucking paws to themselves?'

'He took our fucking horse, the prize money … but I hit him for someone else who couldn't do it, and now can't, nor ever will, right … just fuck off, Milly, any other woman would want that bastard dead on his back for what he did.'

I inhale quickly, feeling a shudder in my soul. I watch Frank get up and jam his cigarette in the ashtray. He leaves then, walking with his torso leaning forward a little, his hands in his pockets. Slams the door behind him.

'I better go after him – Milly – he doesn't mean….' Tom says.

'I know what he means.'

'He means well – you know that.'

I sigh a sigh that comes from my very bones. Tom hurries after his brother and moments later I hear the jeep start up and pull from the yard, rattling the cattle grid on its way out.

Frank doesn't understand that things are on the move. We're on the move. I met Mike the other night in Keadeen. Pat called round and picked me up. He was slightly nervous in himself. He said he hoped he was doing the right thing, with this mediating business. I said I wasn't too sure if he was, and while I was sick at the thoughts of meeting Mike, sick from the apprehension, the revulsion, the fear, the anger, and the hatred, I understood that to achieve my aim I had to meet with him. There was another reason; I wanted to face him, I wanted him to know I no longer feared him.

We need to get away from the farm, from this county. We need a fresh start somewhere else. It's not running away, not just that, I'm always telling Kay, but I want a place from which to start afresh, a place that holds no memories for us. Right now, I'm trying to keep the seams of my family from ripping apart.

Facing him wasn't easy. He is the man who murdered my child. Oh, they call it suicide, or self-inflicted death, but Mike, as far as I'm concerned, fashioned the noose for Adam and led him to his grave. He pushed the buttons. How many other buttons is he pushing or has pushed?

I should have known. There were signs; his excessiveness in bed, the cold way he took me, with little foreplay, making me feel like a thing, not a person, definitely not a woman he loved. Cold, cold, so cold, and yet, for the earlier part of our years together, he was warm and tender. I suppose he got bored with me. He has an insatiable appetite, making love at times that were inopportune – in the loo on a Dublin to Kildare train journey. Thirty minutes of pleasure, coming out to an old man with beautiful blue eyes, who looked us up and down, a small play of disgust on his lips. And then my knickers falling from my coat pocket, my mortification when a woman in an aisle seat said, 'Missus, you dropped your hankie'. Jesus … but he never stopped wanting sex, he was relentless in his pursuit. I should have known. I should have suspected. His coldness was reason enough to cause suspicion. He was only ever truly happy when he was getting what he wanted.

We waited in a lounge with low ceilings and beams, and gas shooting flames up between artificial coals. Deep-piled carpet the colour of blood and paintings of famous racehorses patterning the walls.

Pat sipped his coke, rattled the ice against the glass. He lit a cigarette and bit on his lower lip. 'I'll wait at the counter, over there,' he breathed.

I angled my watch above my eyes. A watch Julie bought in Cyprus, its leather frayed and miniature eyelets in places which once held stitches. 'He's late, isn't he?'

'Give him a few minutes.'

He showed then, stood at the top of a series of steps, tugging at the cuffs of his shirt. When he saw us he gave a small wave of recognition, a grim smile, and ordered himself a beer before joining us.

He sat down. Pat coughed and said what the rules of engagement were – he smiled when he said this, but his stab at humour didn't work – and then said to remember we'd get nowhere if we started to rail against each other.

I watched him go. For moments I felt defenceless in his absence, and then it dawned on me that I wasn't the guilty party here, and that I shouldn't be the weak one, and bucked up my ideas. Mike's a disgusting human being; I wasn't, amn't and will never be what he is.

Mike leaned back in his chair when the barwoman left him down his Guinness, saying he'd pay her later; then he asked if I wanted something, and I said no, and after that he said to give the priest at the counter whatever he was having.

'So?' I said, when she left.

He didn't smoke. I could tell he was taking care of himself. He looked fit and healthy. He had on a blue suit with a garish red tie and a large gold ring with a blue stone on his wedding finger. His slut Angela must have money and no sense.

'I'm selling up the place but the buyer wants the house as part of the deal.'

'How much money are you giving me, straight up?'

'Thirty-five thousand … now, this minute, to leave the place.'

My chin slackened, 'You're joking me – I want half – I want sixty.'

He shook his head, and sipped at his beer, wiping the froth from his lips with a draw of his hand.

I made for my handbag, intending to leave, but he leaned across and grabbed my wrist. My eyes burrowed into his. 'Take your hand off me. *Now*.'

He did but he didn't want to. My wrist ached for seconds and held the red marks of his squeeze. The bastard hurt me. 'If you ever touch me again I'll kill you, Mike, I swear to God I fucking will.'

'Fifty … thirty now, and the rest later … I can't afford any more.'

'I'm not leaving unless I get forty-five now, Mike … I can't afford to.'

He nodded and sighed. He looked rattled and very nervous. 'I can have the money for you in a day or so.'

'Good.'

'I'll give it to Pat for you and the legal papers to sign things over, okay?'

'Okay.'

I could push him for more. Should fight to take him for everything he's got. But that fight simply isn't in me. You need courage and strength and patience to take on a bad bastard, and I'm running on empty. Frank said if I were a boxer I'd have been counted out ten times over. He meant I'd taken so many knocks. Having to sit in Mike's company is making me physically ill. I'm terrified of getting seriously sick. My kids wouldn't survive if anything were to happen to me. I need them in a safe home, so I can ground them; I want to give them hope. I have to get him out of my life and theirs as quickly as possible. I don't want to see him in court, to parade our family mess in public, or to waste money on legal fees – but prison is the proper place for him, along with his own kind of dross. Perhaps later ... perhaps when he thinks he's gotten clean away – in time – maybe the fight will come back to me. Or ... or maybe somebody will just take the fucker out. Look at him. That puss. If I had a knife ... if only. I must, really must get away ... but I'm not going to run from the fucker just yet.

He took a large quaff of his beer and then cracked his knuckles. He regarded me with an icy glare intended to intimidate.

'Why?' I said, evenly.

He heard me, and for a few moments I thought he was ignoring the question, but then he said, 'I don't know – I couldn't help myself – it's an illness. I was abused myself when I was young. That might seem like an old load of shite to you, but I was.'

'By your dad?'

'No ... not by him ... it doesn't matter by who, does it? It happened, that's all I'm going to say about it.'

'Your brother, your sister, your uncle, Mike?'

'I said it doesn't fucking matter.'

I was getting to him, pulling at the stitches of something he thought he had sewn up good and proper.

'Your mother?'

His face burned. Silence. A long brooding silence, full of unspoken things, which I knew in an instant would never be aired. My eyes held his. Did I unearth a truth with a shovel of spite?

'Milly – fuck off, right?'

'I need to know. Adam is dead, and I don't understand why he's dead, Gina has a baby son from you, my husband, Victor's on the brink of either hurting himself or someone else, and as for Morris and Karen … I don't know how they're coping, yet. I spend my days looking for the cracks in them. And it's all your fault, Mike, every damn bit of it. And I don't care who abused you, it's no excuse, in fact you had more of an excuse not to abuse anyone, because you knew what it was *fucking* like.'

He said nothing. Blank face, like a mountain sheeted with snow.

'You heard about the dog, and the rats … Victor?'

'Yes, yeah, I heard.' He spoke in a tired voice, as though every bit of him were winding down.

'I need to get him away from … I mean I'm afraid if I let him see someone he'll be taken away.'

He said nothing, because he could say nothing.

'You've fucked up our lives.'

His 'sorry' was a whimper of near despair.

'How do you live with yourself?'

His quick glance told me it wasn't, and isn't, easy. I sensed that at times he would want nothing more than to be hurt, to have someone punish him physically for his actions. He would see it as being purged for his sins. But what guilt he felt came at him infrequently.

'Do you justify your actions, is that it, make allowances for yourself … your kind do that, don't they, convince themselves there's no wrong in what they did, and what they want to do? And this self-justification enables you to live with yourselves.'

'You have it all thought out.'

'I have very little of it thought fucking out.'

What he said next came low and hard through his clenched teeth, 'I'm sorry for what I did … but not for what I didn't do. I didn't father Gina's baby, right … let's get that straight.'

It was my turn to say nothing.

'I'm a hundred per cent sure,' he said, staring at me from under raised eyebrows.

'How can you so sure. How can you?'

'Just don't bully Gina into going to court over it, right? That's all I say.'

Pat came over. I didn't realise I was crying until he did. He handed me a tissue. Mike said he had better leave and Pat said he should. Then Mike asked if I could keep the kids out of the house tomorrow, as he wanted to clean out the shed of his tools. Pat answered for me, said he'd bring them to the pictures.

I forgot to mention Annie's call to him, and Pat said he'd forgotten too. I didn't even think of it until the next day when I got a late-afternoon call. But Mike knows anyway – what does Annie want me to do? Wring his neck and make him squawk into the phone?

'Annie here....'

'Annie,' I said.

She hung on expectedly.

'Did you...?'

'No ... I'm seeing him today, there's still ... no sign of Ned?' I hated the lie, but it saved a lengthy explanation. I told her I'd remind Mike, again, and then I gave her the hotel's phone number.

'No ... no, no sign,' she said quietly, 'none.' She asked me to repeat the phone number.

Annie runs a swanky antique shop (I suppose they're all swanky) in Cardiff, somewhere off Roath Park. She said Ned went to Ireland to speak with Mike about purchasing a site and hadn't returned. He was also to check in with an antique dealer in Dublin but she rang there too, and he hadn't shown up for the appointment. If she didn't hear from Mike in the next day or two, she was going to the police.

After I put down the phone I wondered where Ned had gotten to. I suppose it shouldn't surprise me what any of Mike's family would get up to. There's Mike, and Ned, a sick-looking man, a sister Ailish, who never married, and another Gina in South Africa who married a Zulu chaplain. Poor Robert died when he was five, from meningitis, and Padraic, who's in the States, left home the moment he turned sixteen. Then there's the father, Des, a quiet man, barrel-chested and freckled-featured, who died three days short of his sixtieth birthday. And Mike's mother, a domineering woman who never accepted losing her children to other people. She's still alive, living in Dunlavin, halfway up a mountain, in her family home. I never let her shadow darken my door. She caused too many rows in our house with her interfering. Unless she's the centre of attention she isn't happy, and the attention she craves is from her sons and daughters. I told Mike to leave her up in the mountains. I just got sick of her and the sight of her made me even sicker. She, Noreen, never liked me. I should have copped on things weren't right with that crowd from the word go. I went in to see her on my own, to have a chat. We weren't going out for long, a couple of months, but it was serious. She made tea and we sat down, in her good room, the one she let no one in, except doctors and priests, and prospective fiancées.

Next thing she thrust a copy of the *News of the World* into my face. 'That's what he has his eyes on all the time, the sort of thing he watches, that's the type he is; I'm sick of him looking at girls in that way.'

A Page 3 girl with breasts like overblown balloons. I was naïve, stupid, and blushed heavily in front of her. I was raging with myself afterwards that I didn't say something, stand up for myself, for Mike, but she was a large woman with a rasp in her throat and an intimidating presence, and if that wasn't enough, well, I was plain shellshocked. I couldn't wait to get out. I'll never forget that deep longing to put a distance between us.

She's a woman who holds grudges, who twists the truth till it blends with her version, who hates to see others get on in life, who sips brandies she freeloads from people, who people shy away from, because she reeks of a malice no one can ever understand. I hear rumours of a strain of madness in her family, and one night, over a cappuccino, I wonder about my own Dad and how he used to say in a low voice that he'd an aunt somewhere, locked up in a mental home. Frank knows. He's a fucker for getting to know things. He says she scraped a man's ball off with her fingernails. You wouldn't know with Frank, sometimes, where he comes from with his stories.

But if it were true and those strains of madness were passed on, and they met up … then Adam hadn't a chance from birth, and neither has Victor, who's bottling up so much anger and frustration inside that I called the counsellor, Hugh Flannery, and said the sessions should begin. How I'm going to persuade Victor to sit in with him is another matter.

Pat drove them to Tallaght, to some picture they asked to see, and a treat of a meal in Eddie Rocket's later. Gina went too, leaving the baby with me. None of them know that Mike – Wonder Bastard – is dropping by.

He drives in in a rented car, hitting the grids hard, and stopping round the back in front of the shed. I watch him from the kitchen. He gets out, looks about and then looks towards the kitchen window, causing me to step back. Using a bolt-cutters he snaps the lock and then drags the double doors apart, one at a time, their ends stubborn against the gravel, like children who resent being parted from each other. Back in his car he eases into the shed, the exhaust billowing a low plume of grey cloud. One of the doors closes of its own accord and the other I see his hand pull behind him.

I've only ever been in the shed once. It smelt of oil and grease, and was cold, with bare walls and large windows, a pit like a grave near the entrance, its thick planks creosoted and bockety. I shiver at the notion of the spiders lurking in there. I want to tell him about Anne's anxiety over Ned, but I already left a message to that effect for him at reception in Keadeen, on Kay's advice. It's his problem. Annie's too. I have enough troubles of my own.

Eric wriggles in my arms and I look down and see Dono wander in from Morris's bedroom. He wants down to play with the pup, claps his hands and I put him into his little hammock chair to let him see more of Dono. I don't like to see Eric creeping along the kitchen floor as I've found him picking up Dono's hairs.

The clock – its ticks are loud. He's been in there for about ten minutes. It's a lapse of another five before he emerges in his car, getting out to close over the doors. He notices me and walks towards the back door, hands buried in his jacket pockets. He smiles his little crooked smile that I used to think was cute, and not twisted, and turns the handle on the door. Locked.

'We need to talk,' he says, his face close to the frosted glass panel.

'I can hear you.'

'Let me in for fuck's sake – I'm not going to do anything. I promise.'

I glance behind me and turn the key in the door. His hand lowers the handle. He stands before me, easing the door shut, turning the key, which sends a ripple of alarm down my spine. Through the window I see that he left his car engine running, the spurt of exhaust fumes like small black clouds.

He has bubbles of sweat on his brow and his pallor is that of someone who was subjected to a bad fright or a bad smell that had flipped his stomach over. I say he looks bad in himself, adding that the guilt must be eating at his insides. With any luck.

He smiles his horrible smile. 'Rats,' he explains, 'a couple in there rotting away ... the poison must have got them.'

He might, like the rats with the poison, burst in front of me. Isn't that what happened to some English king ... ate so much his stomach burst?

He leans against the counter and crosses his legs. The rims of his shoes carry dirt in between the grooves.

'Anne wants you to ring her, I....'

'I got word,' he says quickly.

'Thanks.'

'She's worried about him.' He fans the air with his hands in a mock show of disgust.

'That one is always worrying about something.'

'I suppose she sees Ned as being *someone* as opposed to being *something*.'

'Yeah … right – you heard about the horse?'

'Yes.'

'I got thirty grand for him and another eight in prize money – I'm just waiting for the house documents to come through and we can seal the deal – have you someplace in mind?'

My smile is wooden. He examines his fingernails. Where we go and what we do is none of his concern, not any more. I tell him that, and I tell him he is never to come round my door. A curl of contempt flashes across his face. He sniffles. A cool wave of disgust fills me from head to toe. I tell him it hurts my stomach to see him. He says it hurts his hole to see me.

'What was in the shed?' I ask.

'Tools.'

'Tools – you drove the car into the shed for tools?'

'Heavy tools. Do you want to check the boot…?' He pauses, 'What did you think I was doing in there?'

'You shut the doors after you – when you went in.'

'Force of habit. I thought I would be in there a little longer – but,' he shrugs, 'I hadn't as many tools … did you know the mower is bust and missing its plug?'

'Morris ... he's rough with things... he never said. Then, I shouldn't blame him because no one uses the shed, and I borrowed Tom's mower – so, you must have damaged the mower yourself. Typical of you, isn't it, to blame other people?'

He smiles. 'You're alone here, aren't you?' Our eyes meet at Dono. He yips at Eric.

Our eyes meet at him, too.

'I don't know who he looks like,' Mike says.

'I think it's time you went.'

'I'll be gone in a moment, and you make sure you're out by the end of next week.'

'That's too soon – I need till the end of this month, perhaps the last week in October.'

He takes in the ceiling as though the calendar hangs there and not on the wall behind him. 'No longer than that, Milly, I'm warning you.'

'Your days of warning me about things are over.'

'Are they?'

He moves a couple of paces nearer. And in that couple of paces his normal outwardly appearance changes to one of unbridled anger that makes the veins in his neck and temples stand out.

I hear a voice behind me, 'Yes, they bloody well are, Mike, and you should saddle up and get out, right now.' There is momentary confusion all over his face and then he forces a smile.

'The big one herself ... Kay. Still riding the Padre?'

Kay takes a step forward, in from the hall, her mobile in her hand. 'Yes, Guard, that's right … there's an intruder here. You have the address. Thanks … yes, I can see him. What does he look like? Wait … wait….' She looks past us. 'Do I tell him, Mike, give him your name, your reg. number?'

Mike smacks his lips. The blood oozes from his features. 'I'm going … I'm going,' he says, holding out a hand in a placatory gesture, the other feeling for and finding the door handle behind him. It isn't like him to quit so easily. He's forgotten he locked the door and has to whisk about to flip the key.

He leaves the yard at speed, tyres spinning, spitting gravel. Tools? Only tools? Perhaps. But ones he owed money for, or had borrowed or stolen.

Kay breathes hard and says into the mobile, 'Thanks, John, you're a dear … that's enough of the fantasy for now … yes, yes … give my love to your wife. Good man.'

She smiles. I smile. Did Mike really think I was going to ever be alone with him again?

Kay's a good friend. I've forgiven her for burning Adam's letter. I had to make up my mind about it fairly quickly, too. When I saw Victor's dog that morning in the rain barrel I thought I was going to snap. I needed her then and she was there for me. She's always been there for me. In that respect I've been lucky.

She came over with Pat, leaving her own car in the garage to be serviced, and said she'd stay out of the way if I wanted to speak with Mike. She's a large woman, as large as Noreen, but with none of her badness, her domineering manner. Mike would have seen his mother in her size.

Things are starting to shape up. Pat said the site's in order, full council planning permission, the lot. He brought me to see it last weekend. It's just outside a small village, not too far from the shops, the schools and a new factory that's looking for people. I have an interview lined up. It'd be great to land some sort of a job. The lads are big enough to mind themselves (I hope Victor is going to be okay. He's not done anything abnormal since the time with Rip, although I suspect – I'm trying to make light of what he's done, and might be capable of doing) and so is Karen. Gina can mind Eric. I've had enough of minding babies. I want some of my life back before there's not enough left for me to enjoy it.

11

Victor

October

Morris didn't like seeing the bags of rats I brought into the house. I didn't realise I brought them indoors until I saw the mask of horror on his face. My original idea was to bury them out the back, behind the stables; instead, I ended up throwing the dead rats in the bin and looking in at the mess of red guts and burst rat, I got sick, and later Morris told me that he got sick on top of my sick.

My head goes hot and cold, numb and sensitive, full of ideas, and blank. There's a pain I can't describe because it's not a pain that hurts like a normal headache – it's a dullness, with a searing heat that comes behind my eyes. It's during this *pain* that I do some of the things I think about doing. Pressure, it feels like there's a pressure in my head. I'm afraid it could be a brain tumour.

I sit on a rock at Adam's spot. I see none of the places I usually see because of a mist that shrouds the countryside, a greyish shifting haze allowing a glimpse of the yellow furze on the Curragh, an overtaking truck on the motorway, blinking ambulance lights, a siren tearing at the air, fading.

The barrel of the shotgun tastes cold in my mouth. A squeeze of the trigger and the pressure will be gone. I will lie on the ground with my head lying in bits and the rats will have a feast and the birds will join in too, because they're bastards, rats with wings. I withdraw the barrel; it leaves a taste of grey and smoke in my mouth.

I decide then not to kill myself. It is something I planned on doing after killing the other lad. Now I think I shouldn't die. I have thought this through and I think it is a good plan. If I shoot Dad the papers will publish the reason why and everyone will know what sort of bastard he is, and some, perhaps most, will say I was right to kill him. Either way, I will get to kill the bastard twice, by staying alive. I can imagine Granny Noreen's face, her finger driven up her nose, the way she does, as though she were searching for something to share with you. Dad used to bring me to see her and Aunt Ailish. Morris wouldn't come – he used to hide, or pretend he was sick. Then he got very cute and said he didn't like travelling long journeys, because he got sick.

She sat there, a big slob of a woman, bigger than Kay Walsh, at her nose.

'He's a grand lad … look at him, Mike, you should be proud of yourself.'

Aunt Ailish hanging around, massaging her temples, smelling the scented candles she burned to kill the odour of feet and body that still came through the way shafts of sunlight that pierces cloud banks of grey and black. Granny's not well, she's dying; she doesn't bathe and her eyes are small and piggish and tinged with yellow. Mum says she's been dying for ten years and she tells people things like that so they might overlook her weakness. Mum said *weakness* like she had substituted it for another word which I figured out as wickedness. Mum says she's the source of it all and chopped her off from seeing us about five years ago; none of us miss her too much, or our weird aunt.

I unload the shotgun and am slipping the cartridges into my pocket when I get really cold, so cold I start shivering. Through the mist Adam appears. He stops and stares across at Kildare town, which I can't see. He smokes and then he turns and faces me.

'Cold, isn't it, Victor?'

'Yeah, yeah … it is.'

'So … are you going to join me or what?'

'Why, Adam, why did you kill yourself?'

His eyes are sunken and he looks 'deadly dreadful', like a zombie. I tell him so. 'I'm dead, Victor … are you stupid, how do you think I'm supposed to look?'

'Why, Adam, why are you dead?'

He sits down beside me. He smells of seaweed. Then he shows me his cigarette and says it is good stuff, so I know it isn't tobacco.

'I killed myself.'

'I know that, we all know that – we can't forget – but why…why, why?'

'I had to … but they should all suffer for making me die – one by one, starting with Bollocky Bill, then the others.'

'Jesus, Adam.'

'Don't die angry, Victor – that's all I can say.'

I look hard at the ground. Broken thistle, a cigarette butt, an earthworm. Cold all over. Go away, Adam. Be dead.

'Me – dead, too?'

'Would you want to be alone?'

'No. But I….'

He changes in front of me, right before my very eyes. A brilliant trick,

'Morris….'

He leans forward, has the shotgun in his hand, and his other in my pockets, drawing out the cartridges.

'How did you do that, Adam?'

'I'm not Adam.'

'Morris … Adam's in you. He's taken you over.'

Morris looks shaken up and frightened. He says he didn't want to come up here but that he had to, because had I done anything stupid he wouldn't be able to live with himself. He says he ran so hard his lungs ached; he didn't want to be too late.

I tell him about Adam and then I mention all my ideas, my notions, and the people who raced into mind, people I hadn't seen for years, names I hadn't thought of for years, all fighting for space. Morris is my twin and he is also Adam. He tells me to shut up saying these things, that I'll end up in a mental home, alongside Queenie Travis, who bounces her eye on her palm and sucks on it in her mouth. He's right. I've got to keep my trap shut and do nothing until I get the chance to do what Adam said I should.

I saw him at the races. I got such a fright. I hadn't the shotgun with me. Morris locked it in his wardrobe and hid the key. He told me he was giving the gun to Frank and that he broke up the cartridges with a lump hammer. I told him he was fucking mad; he could have caused an explosion. Morris laughed at that and then he stopped laughing and said I was going around with my eyes half-closed, like I was dosed to the gills on drugs. I said my eyelids were like shutters and my brain wanted them closed, because of all the shit I had to look at every day, shit like him.

Dad didn't see me. Bastard. I felt sick and clammy all over, and when I told Frank I thought he'd freak and go looking for him and save me a job. But he didn't budge, not until afterwards, when he clocked Dad in the Parade Ring, after the dopey horse finished second. Frank said he thumped Dad for Adam, but I think he thumped him over taking the horse. But then, maybe he packed a lot of feeling into one punch.

I'm in no hurry to kill Dad, which means part of me mustn't want him dead at all. It's okay once he stays away from us. Sometimes I look in at myself and I don't know what I'm thinking about at all. When we got back from the races I kept throwing up and Mum blamed the burger Tom bought us, but Morris didn't get sick and he'd eaten two with onions. I don't eat onions. Maybe all this vomiting is Adam telling me to hurry things up and not to let him down.

We are supposed to start school but I let Morris go on his own. I refuse to get in the bus and I go back into the kitchen. I tell Mum I can't face the kids in the school, the way they and the teachers will look at us. I can't handle it. Morris is different (he's Adam, though I didn't say that), he's not bright enough to know when people are cutting the arse off him; either that or he just wouldn't give them the pleasure of knowing they were.

Mum looks at Kay. You'd think that one had a handle on Mum's tongue.

'Okay, Victor, leave it for today – would you like some more breakfast?' Mum says.

A pause, then Mum says, 'Scrambled egg?'

'I make great scrambled egg,' Kay says, her voice sounding very far away.

I didn't mention scrambled egg to her. I'm not fucking talking to her at all. Why is she wearing Granny

Noreen's face? Bitch, that one. Now, she's Kay again. My eyes must be fucked up. Maybe I need a pair like Queenie's. I must have laughed at that because Mum and Kay stared long and hard at me – through their mouths too.

'Bring on the egg,' I say.

Then they relax. Mum's happy to see my appetite is coming back. Lately I feel hungry, very hungry. I eat everything I like and everything *Adam likes*. When Morris bitches over me eating all the Sugar Puffs, I say, 'You're slipping, you used always be at the breakfast table first, Adam.'

He says if I call him Adam again he'll go through me. He is really roused up in himself; then his dog wanders in and he catches me looking at him and picks it up.

'Don't,' he says, his finger stiff as a blade, wagging it, 'fucking dare call him Rip.'

When Kay has gone Mum slips into my room. I am lying on my bed, reading my *Shoot*. I miss playing soccer. I get an urge to go out and start kicking a ball against the shed, then it just goes away. Urges come and go with me, like farts.

Mum says that Father Pat is bringing us to the pictures and to a meal afterwards in Eddie Rocket's. Would I like that?

'Yeah.'

Then she mentions a fellow called Flannery, and it takes me a few seconds to realise that she is talking about the counsellor fellow, that long lad with the old hair and young eyebrows, the one who left Mum his card, and said, *Whenever*.

'Would you like to see him?'

'No.'

'Everyone else is.'

'I'm not everyone else.'

'You're calling Morris … "Adam".'

'A slip of the tongue.'

'You've killed rats – brought them into the house – I had to change the carpet. Can you imagine Gina and Karen if they saw those things?'

'I forgot myself – I thought you'd be delighted to see all those dead rats.'

'Yes … but not in the house.' She falls quiet then. 'And Rip … you don't remember what you did to him, do you?'

I don't. Morris says I drowned him. I didn't. All I remember of that night is tying a cord around his neck and wanting to bring him rat-hunting, and swinging him round and round. And then I stopped, because I didn't want to kill him, but I didn't drown him. I didn't do that. He was alive when I left him … wherever I left him.

'Will you see him … for me … a favour for your Mum?'

'No.'

'You don't have to see him again. Just once, so the others won't get on to me about you not seeing him. After that, I'll tell them you only needed to see him once.'

It seems a good deal. She isn't going to let up, and so I say, 'Okay … once, that's all.'

She sighs in relief. Then she's all chat about the house being built down the country, that I will be sharing a large bedroom with Morris, and we'll have our own toilet and shower. No one will know me in the school and they've a good soccer team as well.

As if I give a fuck.

She makes to go and then stops. 'The shotgun, Victor, Morris told me … Frank wants a loan of it. Have you any more cartridges?'

'No.'

She nods and goes to Eric who is asking for his mother, but she is in the jacks doing up her face. I think she and Karen are going to a disco later on tonight. Bringing each other in case no one else asks them to dance.

I have two cartridges left. Perhaps not enough. One for Dad and, because a shotgun has a wide spray, one to share among everyone in the audience. I hate that Gay Byrne lad. Mum let us stay up and watch *The Toy Show* at Christmas. And all these kids were on dancing and singing and all, and she looked at us and said wouldn't it be great if one of you were musically inclined. I said there were loads of people musically inclined, but they had no talent. Dad said his mother used to play the harp. She was a good harpist. The way he spoke about Granny Noreen made me sick. You'd think she was Our Lady or some other holy person. Mum said she didn't know about her playing the harp but she certainly harped on a bit. We all went quiet, and heard, if not saw, the crack of his hand against her ear. I hate Gay Byrne. He's always saying 'There's one for everyone in the audience', giving out loads of prizes to people. People who were probably his relations, or friends of friends and all.

Father Pat says he's bringing us to The Square in Tallaght. On the way up Morris asks him is he worried about being with us, him being a priest and all.

'Why should I be?' he says.

Gina and Karen giggle. That Gina is stupid. You wouldn't think she's someone's mother the way she carries on.

'Because aren't youse priests getting up on everything?' I say.

Father Pat nods, 'Not all of us.' His face is like the side of a mountain that always gets the worst of the wind. 'Not all of us.'

He sounds like he either passed up the chance to get up on someone, or he was making up his mind if he should or shouldn't.

He doesn't get thick or anything, and I like that about him.

'Are people evil or sick who....' Morris says.

He doesn't know when to let go, ever.

Gina snaps, 'Drop it, Morris, will you? We can talk about that at home.'

Karen says, 'Yeah,' and cuffs Morris's head a little playfully and a little seriously.

We see this film about a volcano erupting and sneezing lava-shit on the people and villages. Then we had chips and burgers in Eddie Rocket's. I like that place with the red seats and the small jukeboxes. Father Pat plays the Drifters' 'Under the Board Walk'. He said he saw them in Monasterevin years ago, in the Hazel Hotel. Some old lady of about sixty threw her knickers on the stage. The truth, he swore – they were that big that the Drifters were looking for a body in them.

We didn't get it.

'Parachute,' he says.

'Stick to saying Mass, honest to Jesus,' Morris says. 'That was a terrible joke.'

The girls go to the toilet. Morris asks if wanking is a sin, and if it is, is it a sin if you don't know you are doing it.

I say, 'How could you not know you were having a wank? Morris, for God's sake.'

Father Pat says, 'Shush now, lads.'

Father Pat doesn't flinch a facial muscle. You'd think talking about wanking was nothing new to him. Morris is certainly asking a lot of questions. Then it comes naturally to him. He was always and forever asking me questions.

'What's this for?'

'What's that for?'

Us

'Do you like Hercules better than Robinson Crusoe?'

'Why do we have to shit … wouldn't it be great if we invented an anti-having-to go-to-the-toilet pill. There'd be no shit in the world, wouldn't there not?'

I told him there'll always be shit, for forever and a day in the world. It was a metaphor, but he didn't understand.

Father Pat is cool. He tells Morris he'll explain later but not to worry about it because he won't go blind, or deaf, or it won't fall off or wear out.

I think Morris is asking people the questions he used to ask me. I feel a little sad that's how things turned out, and when I linger on how close we once were, a bar of heat turns on in my head and I go very quiet deep down, way deep down.

I feel as though I've passed a point. I feel as badly in myself as the morning Adam was found. The emptiness – I feel like a desert inside. The sands are cold at my feet and the sun is warm on my face – and all about me the air is yellow, as though poisoned.

We reach home late and it is dark, with the stars bright and a cut of moon lying on its back. Father Pat says 'Goodnight', declining Mum's offer of tea, saying he has to get back because he has to relieve a priest of duty. Kay travels with him. She is all smiles, telling Pat about the guest who dropped in. She says it in a low voice but not low enough. I know Mum is raging with her, because she doesn't want any of us to know that Dad has shown his face, in here, in this house. My head gets warmer.

I go out back with Morris, who brings Dono outside for his goodnight slash against the rain barrel that his brother was found dead in. Frank and Tom moved the barrel beside the stables, turned it upside down and emptied it. They're going to hire a skip to clear out all the rubbish before we move. Dono gets playful and runs towards the shed where the blackness swallows him. The doors are open. That bastard had gone in there, had probably entered the office where he had started doing his thing with Adam, in that poky office of his. *Adam, mix the paint – that's right – black with white to get grey – just stir, good boy.*

Adam didn't tell me how things would end but he told me how it all began.

I shout at the darkness, I keep shouting and shouting, till the shouting becomes screaming, and I scream for the darkness to leave me alone, to leave us alone, and all I remember is the shooting pain in my temples and the grin of moon as I fall to the ground.

That is all I remember. I don't know what I shouted and why I screamed. I think it was at the past. It couldn't have been at the future – could it?

12

Gina

October

His voice carries, touching a nerve in the lot of us. When we reach him he is still screaming. The sight of him, the pain in his voice, chills me to the marrow. A bitterly cold wind is rising, carrying a smell of rain. Turning him from the shed we guide him inside. Once he hits the kitchen Victor switches off his mouth. Eric starts to cry. He would. Victor grinds his teeth. We sit Victor on a fiddleback chair, the one missing two rods, and watch as he rocks himself back and forth, his eyes transfixed on the range and its shimmering turf heat. Doc Fleming comes around and injects him with a sedative, whispering in the hall to Mum his dark fears concerning Victor.

Morris is shocked. He says Victor just started shouting out of the blue. *Stop! Stop! Don't! Leave him alone ... leave him alone!*

Then he started screaming.

We put Victor to bed and leave a bedside light on for him in case he wakens and the darkness triggers him off again.

'Is there no end to this?' Mum says over tea in the kitchen when the others have gone to bed.

'There will be, Mum.'

She rakes her fingers through hair that needs cutting and styling. Lighting up a cigarette, she draws heavily and holds the smoke for moments before exhaling.

'The sooner we get out of here, the better,' she says.

Then she speaks about the house, that Pat had the builders working full steam to have it built within the three weeks Dad had given us to get out. He said he would get down at the weekends to lay a few blocks himself. It should be ready, weather permitting, in time. She told me about the money Dad gave her, how Pat had arranged a small Credit Union loan for her to make up the shortfall to meet the building expenses and Kay said she was giving her her old car as soon as she bought a new one, a Honda Civic. Things are looking up, and maybe she'll land the job – fingers crossed.

Mum goes very quiet, parks her cigarette on the ashtray, and says, looking at me straight on, 'I was talking with your Dad … you know that?'

'Ah, yeah, you've just told me, and about the money he coughed up.'

I get very uncomfortable but try not to show it. I am always uncomfortable at the mere mention of his name.

'Gina ... he,' she shakes her head. Dandruff snows on to the shoulders of her grey cardigan. 'Gina, he says the baby isn't his.'

Taking a deep breath I sigh a tortured sigh, 'I don't want to talk about him, Mum, really.'

'Will you let me report him to the guards?'

'No ... no.' I turn my head, exaggerating an interest in my toes.

'If not for your sake, then for Adam's, don't let him get away scot free.'

This isn't Mum talking. This is Mum fishing. The real Mum doesn't want me going near the courts, to save our name, to save us the ordeal; she simply doesn't want to put us through the whole legal system. She saw it as sparing us, from our own words, from men in wigs, from strangers, from the media, from everything.

I know her well enough to know this is what she really wants, a funeral for our past.

'If you think I should, Mum ... I'll go, I'll go ... I will. I'll tell the guards and go to court.'

She says nothing, just resurrects her cigarette and gives it a red eye.

'You have to want to do it yourself.'

'I do, Mum, honestly, but ... but I just want to get on with my life. That's all I want to do, nothing more than that.'

She nods. I want to tell Mum something else. I don't want to move down the country, not to where she intended living, in a pokey village. I want to live in a town or a city, not any place that'd remind me of this place. I don't want the smell of a farmyard anywhere near me. There are other reasons: I don't want to live in the same house as Victor the Timebomb. I'd sooner live on my own with Eric in a flat, find a job and get on with things. You can't plan the past, only the future, and yet sometimes all I think about is the past. How can I forget? Eric is there to remind me.

How can I forget the nights of fear, the days I felt so dirty and disgusted with myself that I thought of slitting my wrists? How can I forget Adam's kindness, the strength he gave me to carry on, giving me his strength, too much of his strength, leaving none for himself. My pregnancy, the straw that broke the camel's back. I'm not going to give in, for my sake, for Eric's, and as a mark of respect for a brother I loved, who helped me live through dark days, when my skin itched from the feel of my father's fingers.

Mum changes tack then, going on about Annie ringing looking for Dad, to ask him about Ned, his brother. She falls quiet and tears form in her eyes.

'Mum,' I say, moving to her, taking the cup from her hand. 'Mum....'

There are no words. We just hold each other and don't let go until Eric begins to cry in his cot and I answer his calls, heavy-hearted, knowing Mum has aged twenty years ahead of her time and that Victor is going to add another ten, and that we are all to blame, even Mum herself, because she slept at her post, as Uncle Frank might say, and didn't keep night watch.

The next day Victor gets his breakfast in bed. He doesn't like toast crusts. Karen says he looks awful pale in himself. Morris sits on the edge of his bed, eating the crusts his brother doesn't want.

'Are you all right, Victor?' Morris says.

'Yeah … what happened.'

'You blacked out on us,' I say by the door so I don't have too far to walk in case he tells me to leave.

'I don't remember.'

Dinner smells drift in, the smell of boiled ham, new Wexford potatoes and cabbage. Morris says Victor has broken the record in our house for lying on in the mornings because it is now almost two o'clock. Breakfast meets dinner.

Victor lifts his arm and lets it flop. 'I've no fucking energy at all.'

'The doctor will be around later on,' I say.

'Doc Fleming?' Victor says.

'Doctor Doom,' mutters Morris.

I leave them there. Victor always makes me feel as though I'm to blame for everything. He frightens me. I am thinking of how much he frightens me when Karen says, 'Will we go to a disco tonight? Pharaoh's, Snaffles or Nijinski's? We should have gone last night, only for you know who.'

I say no, and then yes, and then no again, before finally saying yes. Mum doesn't mind, says she doesn't mind. I say that I won't make a habit of her minding Eric or take her for granted. 'That's right, Gina, you won't.' She says it with no hardness in her tone.

We dance a lot and Karen meets up with a boy she knows who buys her a drink, taking her away to an alcove seat. I think that one has it planned. We came out here in a taxi and pre-booked the return journey. Nijinski's is out in the country a bit, off the army rifle ranges and right across from where Mel Gibson shot his battle scenes for *Braveheart*. I saw him once. He was gorgeous.

I dance most of the night. Some of the fellas are okay. One smells of drink but not enough to drown out his bad breath and another smokes a joint. A lad called Brian tries to shift me. He tries very hard. He almost begs. He isn't good-looking, carries a little raised nose showing his nostril's cave-like openings. I want to have a good time and just dance the night away, sink a beer or two and a couple of vodkas. Unwind. I don't want romance. He's from Naas and works at the horses as a farrier. God, I think he is going to bore me to tears with his chat about different types of horseshoe. He just talks on and on, one word after the other, until I say, 'See you,' with a lot of muscle in my tone, leaving him there, middle of the dance floor, like a pig after falling off the back of a lorry.

He arrives over afterwards as I am handing in my ticket to collect my jacket. A sour-faced bitch with chin-terracing drops cigarette ash on the back of my hand.

She says sorry but she doesn't mean it. She just says it so I won't say anything. Karen, the wagon, tells me she's all right for a lift home. We exchange words and Terrace-Head is licking up every word. Like a child picking up a spill of sweets.

'Karen – who is this guy?'

'Some lad I know.'

'Has he a name?'

'Of course he has a name. And it's a not made-up one – like the phantom Terry who got you pregnant.'

I feel like pulling every hair out of her fucking head. How can she piss off in a car with a fella after what she's being through with men? All they want is the one thing; they might be nice upfront, and chatty, decent and kind, but all they really, really want is to climb between your legs. That's all. When I want a man I'll get one and use him before he uses me, like Kay Walsh does to her married friend, keep him on a leash.

Brian waits. I look at Karen leaving through the exit doors, the green 'e' missing from the neon sign above the door. Half past one – the taxi should be here any minute. What'll I tell Mum? Karen's at the dentist? Gone riding? Bitch. As I make to move I know by Brian that he is definitely waiting for me and is definitely bursting to tell me something.

'I heard,' he says, a drunken leer on his face, 'that you only like daddies.'

I tear his face with my fingernail. The bouncers pull me off him, and put me and my jacket outside. Leaning against the wall I break out crying; the hurt, the alcohol and the bastards talking in the disco about me and my family. Fuckers. Talking about me and my family.

Everyone has a skeleton in their closet. I just have too many bones in mine, so many I can't close the door after the initial spill. And people are like dogs – gossip hounds. It shouldn't bother me what they say, but it does. It does.

The taxi driver squints my way, lowers his window and puts his half-bald dome out a little. Then his lips tighten. He mumbles something I can't hear and drives away, rattling the loose bars in a sheep grid, indicating left. I'm trouble in his eyes. A young one with drink. Double trouble.

Three miles to home. Jesus. Not a light a hundred-metres after Nijinski's. Some minibuses are pulling away but they are heading deep into culchie land, and taking right turns instead of the left I need. A few people lean against a chip van, under its slim awning. I think about buying a bag of chips just to kill the time and keep an eye out for another taxi, but I spot Brian forking out money to the Chippie and I swing through the wicket gate from the grounds and step onto the road. The last thing I need is to see him and the red mark down his cheek. I imagine I have some of his flesh under my nail, but I don't. The notion sickens my stomach.

My jacket's black, and my ski-pants are black, and my shoes, even my pop-socks are black. I'm at one with the night, I think, which sounds like a bit of poetry, or at one with the grave. I walk along the edge of the Curragh Plains, taking care because of horse divots and sheepshite, and dips and rises in the ground. Now and then I meet a furze bush and go around and take in the deep scent from its spiky brambles.

I'm mucked up to the knees. I'm going to kill that bitch when I get home. I could walk the road but in my garb I'd be run down, and because I'm a woman some bastard or bastards might stop and whisk me into their car. If I were a fellow I could stroll home happily, half-locked, with no fear of a pair of women jumping out of a car to whisk me away. Men are so fucking sick.

Adam's grave. Jesus, it's cold. I could have done with another vodka. Sheep maa at my presence and hurry away. I'm not a sheep-shagger, I tell them. They hang snatches of wool on the furze in their haste. They don't believe me. Proper order, girls. I've heard about men being at the sheep. *Men*. Again. Dirty bastards. The girls at the convent used to slag me off about coming from the Curragh. All those sheep, the horny bastards chasing after them, coming into the disco at the weekends, looking for a change of wool. Men. DIRTY BASTARDS. I hate them all.

Ahead of me a dog starts barking so I take to the road. A pair of small windows in a pair of small caravans light up. I smell woodsmoke, see the dying embers of burning sticks, the familiar Hiace vans. My heart misses a beat. My heels clobber the road. A mile down, a left turn at the Rising Sun Pub, a tongue of footpath then and some streetlights. A phone booth. Thank Jesus. He just has to be a woman. I laugh at the notion. I should be going back to school but I'm a mammy. In two months time it'll be Christmas. Last Christmas, around then, the season for giving, it happened. His shadow across my door, his shadow covering me, his shadow in me.

A card phone. Shit. I should have brought Mum's mobile with me. She offered but I was afraid of losing it or having it robbed. The road beyond the community hall yawns dark and lonely. There are a few stars in the sky but more cloud, shifting black cloud. I begin to walk. The heels of my shoes going *tip, tap, tip, tap*.

We went to Adam's grave last week, Mum and I. Our first time since the funeral. I was struck by all the graves that surrounded Adam's. So many new ones in eight short months. We cleared away the withered wreaths and flowers and touched his name on the grey headstone, put flowers in vases and tried hard to pray for him. It's very hard to pray. You pray and pray and pray for a father to stop loving you the way he shouldn't love you, and when all those prayers aren't answered, you know whoever's there isn't listening or is as dead as Adam.

Pitch dark. The only sounds the sweep of easy wind and downy flake – Robert Frost.

Jesus. I've got goose-pimples riding goose-pimples. Nice one, Gina girl, putrid mind that you have.

There's a light on outside Queenie's house. I walk a little quickly past her gate, refusing to look that way, trying hard not to, but hearing the wind rustling the branches of her apple-trees and imagining the creak of a rope, like clothes heavy on a line about to snap.

'The state of you!' Mum says.

I almost fall in my hurry to shut the door behind me.

'I've been worried out of my mind, Gina.'

'Where's that bitch?'

Mum says, 'She's in bed, sulking over what I said about leaving you behind. Why?'

'I was going to fucking eat her, that's why.'

'She came home an hour ago. Some fella left her home. Nice lad … came to the door.'

Jesus, Mary and Joseph. I sigh long and hard, losing the fear that gripped me during the walk. I wrap my fingers round the mug of tea Mum hands me and stare through the window at nothing, only darkness. Mum whispers my name. I know by her tone she doesn't want me going deep and distant on her.

Mum smiles. 'You smell of sheepshite and burnt wood. What sort of date had you?'

I tell her everything, leaving out Queenie Travis's place and the rustling of her trees, the tweaking of a rope.

We say goodnight and I head to the bathroom, feeling cold and tired and praying Eric won't waken. But he's a good sleeper, considering it's a disturbed house. In the hallway I notice that Morris's door is ajar. He must be feeling brave in himself again. I suppose there's no Dad, no … I had Adam's name on the brink of my tongue but he was nothing like Dad.

Dono is a short way down the hall, pawing at the kitchen door, whimpering.

'Shush, boy, shush, go easy.' I let him in the kitchen, and he moves his snout to the lino for the patch of newspaper Morris spreads for him at night. I look away. Morris! A fucking single sheet isn't enough for Dono to piss on. He's growing … he needs a few spreads of paper. When he's finished, he makes for Morris's bedroom, wagging his tail, nosing his way inside to check on his master before settling down on one of Mum's old cardigans. My heart jack-knifes. I swallow air, can't scream. Victor stands outside his own bedroom door, wavering on his feet. He wears a red T-shirt with Tweety Bird on it and blue boxers. 'Victor?'

He stares straight ahead at a painting of a wood, and a girl by a stream tying up her hair. A foot forward, he starts for Morris's room. Dono's whimpering is loud and grows louder. A bark. A show of his small white teeth. Is it true – what Mum said – I thought she was teasing – is Morris brushing the dog's fucking teeth?

'Jesus, Ma…Ma…Ma…' Morris says.

He's a sheep. *Ma, ma*. His bedroom light spills shadows onto the hall carpet. Karen opens her door and comes up to my shoulder, covering her love bite. 'Get Mum, Karen. Go on.'

Mum's hands fly to her ears as though in an effort to keep her head in place. She's so good, so concerned for us all. I see that in her eyes, in the loving way she whispers to Victor, as she leads him back to his room.

Sunday, and the night carries away most of last night's cloud, allowing the sun to pour in through the window, shining up a column of dust that intrigues Eric. I am tired. He is hungry. If I wasn't a mother, I could lie on in bed all day, and perhaps think about Brian, the way he looked at me. Perhaps, in different circumstances, we would have kissed and got close, but if there's any advantage in what I am, and in my present circumstances, it is that I got to know Brian fairly quickly, that his outwardly show of the 'sound guy' was just a thin shell of a lie.

Victor is gone. Not gone walking the countryside in his underwear, but gone as in run away. A fully planned escape.

Mum's agitated voice reaches me from Morris's bedroom.

'I don't know where he's gone, Mum,' Morris says. 'How would I know?'

Joining them in Victor's bedroom, I think how broken-up Mum looks, the way the lines are carved deeply about her eyes and along her forehead. Morris says there is a rucksack missing, and Adam's old tent, and a sleeping bag. Then he shuts up and looks hard at us. Panic in his eyes, a quiver in his jaw muscles.

'He took the shotgun, Mum.'

I say nothing. The missing shotgun alarms them but not me. Victor's bed is made up, neat and tidy, pillow fluffed, the creases still in place on his Ireland World Cup 1994 duvet, where I hadn't leaned too heavily on the iron. The morning we went into Adam's room, the morning we were told of his death, we saw that his bed was made up. The lads aren't usually so hot about making their beds. It's a statement of sorts.

A farewell and fuck-ye gesture, it reads like. Or maybe just a farewell.

Hugh Flannery is due to start his counselling today. Sunday's a free day for him.

When she comes over, Kay Walsh rings him and cancels the whole thing again. Just tell Milly whenever she's ready, she says he said.

Frank calls. Mum takes his call. She hasn't time to say anything else other than 'Hello?'

He has something to tell her and will be around later on to break the news. She eases home the phone and tells us what he said. Going away?

'Why didn't you tell him about Victor?' Kay asks.

'I'm sick of having to run to people over the goings-on in this family. Sick and fucking tired of it. So sick.'

Father Pat is down at the new house, adding bricks. On the quiet, Kay asks me to ring Frank and tell him.

'The guards?' I say.

'Useless shower … don't talk to me. I'll wait till Guard Richards comes on the afternoon shift. He – he –'

She doesn't finish. She is about to say that he was involved in Adam's case. *He'd know the ropes.*

As the percolator spits and hisses, Morris says that Victor has taken the variety pack of cereals with him, that he has robbed the place of food. He says this a couple of times and once too often because Mum shouts at him to stay quiet.

After a spell of quietness Morris says almost inaudibly, 'Robbing our food means he isn't going to kill himself, like Adam, doesn't it?'

I say, 'Yeah ... he's just gone to get some air.'

Morris. You can't be sarcastic with him. It just flies over his head. The phone. Every time it sounds we jump. We get better starts than any Olympic sprinter and we don't need drugs. Though perhaps a cocktail of fear and anxiety is a drug?

Kay answers, her features puzzling over and then brightening, 'No, Annie ... I'm Kay Walsh, I'm afraid ... yes, that's right ... she can't come to the phone right now.'

Mum's eyes reach for the ceiling. Dad. All his crowd must be the greatest wasters ever born. There's Uncle Ned, after running off and leaving Annie. If he's anything like Dad, she should let him run, run till his heart gives out, although black hearts live longest; it's the devil in them, and the owners get great mileage.

Victor's out there, in the fields, walking in sunshine, his mind gone, focused on whatever it is he is focused on. Carrying a shotgun for which he has no cartridges, so Morris says. Morris is angry with himself for leaving the key in his wardrobe door. A pure dope, he says. No one disagrees. Victor just put his hand in the wardrobe and took the shotgun.

Jesus – thank God – he didn't use it on us. He wouldn't. He's fucked up – he simply doesn't have a clue what he's at, but he wouldn't hurt any of us. I think.

Morris says he didn't think Victor … well, his twin was sick in bed.

'You didn't think, Morris – you never do. But start thinking now. Where would he have gone?' I say.

Morris lowers his head and I know he's thinking hard about where Victor might have gotten to. But I don't think he'll find the right answer.

13

Morris

Mid October

I don't know why Victor needs the tent. Last summer we got Adam to put it up in the front garden because we couldn't and Victor lost his temper and started kicking at the canvas and throwing the wire pegs and aluminium poles about. So, I imagine he's in a wood somewhere, kicking the shite out of the tent and screaming because this peg or that pole won't fit for him. Mum says he's easily frustrated.

He took my favourite cereals too. I should expect nothing else from him. After all, he's the very one who eats the last biscuit in the house, the one everyone else would leave for someone else to eat. I got on to him once, as he stuffed the last mini Mars bar in his mouth.

'Victor – you're selfish, you know that – you eat the last of everything in the house.'

'Someone has to. I don't mind being the volunteer.'

'Mean, it's mean.'

'No, it's not. Someone has to eat the last one. No one else does, do they? No, it's always left up to me. Leave the last one, me hole. Someone had to be the first-born person in the world, isn't that right? And someone will have to be the last dead person in the world, isn't that right?'

'So?'

'So what – are you thick, are you?'

'So what are you telling me, Victor, that it's okay to be greedy?'

'Look, if Robinson Crusoe had two bags of chips … are you with me so far?'

I said nothing. He was beginning to more than annoy me.

'And if he ate his bag of chips, right, and that left another bag, right? And Man Friday says, "You ate them, Boss, work away, I don't like chips," what would Robinson do, eh? Answer me that. Go on.'

I knew but said I didn't.

'He'd ate them before they went cold, that's exactly what he'd do. He'd ate every chip right down to and including the last one. Why? Because he'd know no one else wanted it, that's why.'

Suicide, who's the first person to commit suicide – his name? The Bible tells us the name of the first murderer, why not the name of the first *suicider*. Maybe it does, but no one ever mentions his name, the way people don't really like talking about suicide. I must ask Father Pat, he might know his name. Not that it's important, it's just being curious.

A tent, a sleeping bag, a torch, some food, a shotgun – that's what Victor has with him. I wonder how he got over the first night. I imagine him in his sleeping bag, the tent lying over him because he can't erect it and has gotten thick. Lying there, his teeth chattering away, his eyes gone lazy in themselves – like they were looking at you on half-power or something – taking in the stars, his mind ticking away, thinking up crazy ideas.

I miss him, the old Victor. I miss Adam too and Aunt Julie. But Adam and Julie are dead and the way I miss them is different to the way I miss Victor, though in a sense it feels like he's dead also.

Uncle Frank said life can kill you before you die, and I think he's right. Queenie Travis would agree, too. Then, she agrees with everyone about anything. Frank came over yesterday morning and said he was leaving for Lebanon next week. He shrugged and said the time was right for him. If he let things dilly-dally he'd end up not going. Fatima is a fresh start for him, a new life and probably a new wife. Mum nodded and found a smile somewhere from him, taking it from her stock room of old memories. He and Tom set off at lunchtime, searching the fields and the river's banks, maybe keeping one eye on the river itself, and returned when it got dark. Frank stayed over. Tom couldn't. He has horses to feed, water and exercise. Horses don't give a shit what's going on around them, once it isn't happening to them, Tom said. Mum said there are a lot of people like that.

I'm kicking the ball about in the front garden when Guard Richards drops by. Mum opens the door to him and lets out a scream. Kay goes as a pale as the moon and Tom says, 'What, Doug? Spit it out for fuck's sake, come on!'

'I'm enquiring about Mike – I he – '

I think Tom is going to thump the guard or take a heart attack, his cheeks flare so red.

'Do you know Victor's missing?' he says. Belligerently.

That's a word he uses himself. He's all the time saying, 'That's a belligerent fucker, that lad.'

'Yes … have…?'

'Some crowd of fucking eejits ye lot are,' Tom says.

Kay edges Tom away before his tongue lands him in gaol. The guard's high cheekbones flush. He takes off his cap. There's a crack along its peak. His brown eyes mist and he says he is sorry for not thinking, that he should have rung before appearing on the doorstep in uniform, and that yes, he has some of his men out searching the woods. But he needs to speak with Mike in relation to his brother's whereabouts, as his wife Annie has reported him missing.

That guard scares the heart out of us. Mum can't stop shaking in herself and Kay says she feels sick in her stomach, that the fright she got soured the cream eclairs in her belly. Tom keeps looking at the guard, biting his lower lip, in the kitchen, where Doug Slug sits on the edge of the sofa asking questions about Ned, trying to pinpoint the date when we last saw him. Mum and Kay tell him about Dad driving the car into the shed. The guard nods, says he'll check the shed. He says it in a quiet, confidential tone as though his checking the shed is serious business – he says it like he expects to find evidence. Dad murdered Ned? A body? Clues? Jesus.

'Was there an argument between them?' Doug asks.

I don't tell him about the row I overheard between Dad and Ned. Even if the guards are the good guys – it's hard to explain – but I have a reluctance to tell them things. It comes from deep within. Then, I have a reluctance to tell anyone the whole truth about truths.

Did Dad kill Ned? That's what I ask myself, that's what Doug is implying under all his official lingo: *We don't have much to go on at the moment* thing. I don't know why I didn't tell him about the row between Dad and Ned; after all, I hate Dad, every gut that makes him up, I hate him. But I'm not too fond of Guard Richards either. Not after he frightened us and scattered our thoughts to the wind.

Mum mentions Granny Noreen and where she lives, and the guard says he'll take a spin out that direction and check, but he would hardly run back to his mammy, he says, would he? Those boys love their mammy, Mum says. She says it in a way that has layers of other meanings, like the stories I read in my English textbook, which the English teacher is always asking us to reflect upon as to what the author really means.

I like my writers to be direct, straight out and bold. The English teacher, Max is his name, said that's fine, but what if the writer wasn't allowed to write critically of a government, for instance – he would have to disguise his meaning, which could have other meanings. No wonder Victor got to thinking that Robinson Crusoe and Man Friday were gay. Nothing in life is simple or is at it appears. And I suppose that's for fucking sure.

Take Dad. He was on the Athletics Committee and fundraised for the soccer and rugby teams all over Kildare. You wouldn't think it of him as he sold little paper flags on flag days outside churches, that he couldn't keep his hands off things, private things, which weren't his to touch. He was in a lot of clubs, doing favours for friends but always having disagreements with them over money going missing. Victor used to say he should be in government.

Father Pat got it wrong about Dad too, asking him to play Jesus Christ one Good Friday. Mum wasn't really friendly with him then, that came later, through Kay Walsh.

'You'd make a fine Jesus,' Pat said.

'God, I wouldn't,' Dad laughed.

'Errah you would – the Cross isn't heavy – you'll only have to carry it a bit of the way.'

Adam said, 'And sure couldn't the rest of us drive the nails into his feet and hands.'

Father Pat got uncomfortable when he saw no smile on Adam's face.

'Shure we'll leave it so … I'll ask Manny … round up the usual Manny, the reliable Jesus, eh – the only thing is he'll be coughing and spluttering his way to Mount Calvary and saying "Merciful Jesus" over and over again.'

None of us smiled. That day Pat couldn't wait to get out. *Pontius Pilate.*

I've only been to school a couple of days since the term started. We missed the last two months of last term and will probably miss most of this one too. Mum says we won't get a proper start on things till we move to our new house. I'm looking forward to getting out of here, to a new school and new faces who might look at you because you were a stranger in town but not as though you went around with your mickey hanging out.

I go for a walk. I just go, not even bringing Dono along. I take my school bag because it holds a Mars Bar, half a bottle of cola and some scones. I make for the hill.

Kildare looks lovely today, basking in sunlight.

That first morning back in school I felt like ET. It's hard to face everyone, even if they are great and say nice things. I think they're afraid of saying a wrong word in case I do what Adam did. But Dildo, he's my friend who used to cycle out to swap comics and video games most Saturdays (I think he had a crush on Karen more so than my comics and games), tapped me on the shoulder and started speaking with me as though nothing had happened. During a drop off in the conversation I said, 'Dildo, why didn't you call round?'

'I didn't like to – I don't know why – it's not because of Adam or that, you know, what your Daddy did to Gina, getting up on her and all, and the baby and that.'

'It wasn't?'

'No … do you think he was at Karen…?'

'I don't know – why don't you ask her?'

He knew he was making me mad but was blind as to how he was doing it.

'I mean, hey – my dad says it could happen to anyone – he almost rode our granny one night he was so drunk. It would have been an accident like. I swear to God. Have you seen my granny.…'

On and on he went. Not once did he ask about Victor, where he was, how he was doing. Nothing. He just wanted to talk. In the end I left him there, telling him he was rightly nicknamed. I left school early, walked home. It rained and I got pissed on, soaked to the skin. A couple of cars, with people I know to see in them, drove past pretending they didn't know me to see.

Queenie was out, clipping her hedge, her sopping privet hedge, as wild as her own grey hair. The rain had stopped but the sky was full of it, waiting to start up again. A brilliant rainbow, the closest one I've ever been to, stood in the field across from Queenie's house. It coloured a Friesian cow and trailed down a small hill. The sight was a small treasure. A thick band of delight.

'Isn't it lovely, son?' she said, joining me.

I didn't turn about. I'd just farted and I hoped she had no sense of smell.

'Yeah, it is.'

'You're a brother of the boy who....'

'Yeah ... I better be going now.'

It started to rain.

'Why don't you come inside, until the rain blows over.'

I didn't want to go in but I ended up going in. I wondered if Adam felt the same way about dying – he didn't want to do it but he had to? A few months ago I'd have been too scared of Queenie to chat with her. Now I don't mind her glass eye, and I don't mind her. I know she'll agree with whatever I say. It's part of her madness, so Uncle Frank says.

On the hill I drink my cola and eat the bar. I'm sitting on the rock Adam used to sit on. I thought I might find Victor here. But no – I guess he doesn't want to be found. Queenie ...Victor ... mad things.

She made some tea and buttered me a scone which I didn't eat because she'd dirty fingernails. Her tea wasn't great either: loose tea-leaves circled my milky mug. We sat across from each other in her small sitting-room, me on a couch with lace cloths on the back and arms, and she on an armchair that held a dark patch against which she rested the back of her head.

She was nearest the door. She trapped me with her tongue, talking rapidly, riddling me with shite-talk.

'I remember, God when was it, years ago. moving here, and your mammy's family lived on the Curragh, and then she got with Mike Nugent, your daddy. God, the Curragh was a great place in those days, neighbourly, everyone looked after each other, not like today, sure they're pulling all the veranda quarters down, and didn't I go for a walk the other day and saw a new skyline of hills I never saw before, right where your mammy's house used to be. I never liked your dad's crowd – strange fish, a different set of gills to the rest of us....'

On and on she went, breathing names I never heard of: Horace Pink, Prince Monolulu, Biddy this and Biddy that, Colonel Mumbles the mad officer who used to dance naked in the snow; she never stopped. And when she finally did, she laid her hands on her lap and shook her head. She closed her good eye, leaving the other one open, which I found unsettling, and more so when I put my cup on the tray, and she said, 'More tea?' the good eye shooting open, as if the other had woken it for being bad-mannered.

'No thanks – I better be off.'

She gave me a slight nod. 'You're a good boy. Don't go near my orchard – if you want apples I can get some but don't go out. You could have an accident. A boy had an accident out there a while ago. I saw him, you know, he fell off the tree, and the rope was tight on his neck, and he was trying to pull himself up, and he kicked this way and that, and I held his legs and tried to lift him but I'm not strong any more and couldn't, and he was panicking and kicking, and then I left him, I had to go and get a knife to cut him down, and when I came back he had stopped kicking, and I just left him there – I was very sick after that, worrying about that poor boy. I don't go in the orchard any more. Jesus knows I can't. Sometimes at night I still hear him, his gasps, his kicks against the tree, the moon on his terrified face. My window breaking … I forget when that happened but it happened the same night. I got slivers of glass in my hair, I was combing it out for weeks.'

Her black cat with the horrid green eyes came through her door, in through a panel where there was no glass and sat at Queenie's feet. Now Queenie looked like a witch.

I knew the window she spoke of, there were a pair of finger-marks on the new putty and on the glass where I saw the grooves of a thumb. I like the smell of fresh putty. I made to move, but delayed for a few moments and then I said I had to go, putting aside the notion of asking her if I could see the tree from which Adam jumped, again. Queenie said goodbye and insisted on putting a few scones in a bag for me to take home.

Outside, I pulled the door shut behind me and walked as quickly as Queenie had spat her words. The rain fell in spots and the rainbow was gone. Bits of magic don't last forever in life, you enjoy them when you can. I was glad I stopped to look, though I thought it a pity that Queenie came along. When you really want to be left alone it appears you never are, and when you really need someone you're left alone, like poor

Queenie, who's really lonely, who doesn't like being alone with her thoughts because they're probably what makes her mad.

Adam. I wish she hadn't told me those things. I had this idea in my head that he just jumped and died. I didn't think about what happened in between – the way his weight and the speed of his drop tightened on his neck, squeezing the air out of him. Adam changed his mind. It might have been during the drop, before the rope bit into his neck, but he changed his mind. Had he seen a reason to live, just when it was too late? That's fucking life for you. He shouldn't have jumped. I tell him that every night in my prayers. *You shouldn't have jumped, Adam, you should have thought more of us, more of Victor, and less of what Dad and you had done.* Perhaps Adam had a real fear of ending up like Dad and he didn't want to cause any young fella the pain he himself lived through. It was a little of that and a little of something else I don't let myself think about too much. I'm like Dad in *that way* – I can shut things out.

I decide to head back. The sun's gone and it has turned cold. I walk through a bed of yellow leaves, rustling them, drowning out my thoughts.

Dono doesn't know what to make of us. He tilts his head and takes us in with his sad brown eyes. I don't think he realises he's one of us now, more so, I think, than baby Eric, who's still handed round like a hot potato. Rounding the back he comes up, wagging his tail and brushing against my leg. In my bedroom, I throw Queenie's scones, mouldy after days, in the bin along with my Mars wrapper and empty cola bottle. I can hear a lot of talking going on in the sitting-room and catch the smell of cigarette smoke. Kay and Mum talking again. About the night the girls went dancing and Victor went sleepwalking, and then later woke up and left us, robbing all round him, heading off on his own, into the darkness that he feared. Taking the shotgun Frank was meant to bring away.

Entering the kitchen no one says anything to me. Karen's yapping away, her arse planked on the edge of the table. I don't know how many times I've got on to her over doing that. Frank and Tom read newspapers and smoke. Gina nurses Eric on her lap. He loves creeping, and soon he'll be on the supplementary diet of worms they say I was on when I was his age ... the notion of an earthworm wriggling in my mouth chills my spine. 'Get off the table – we've to eat our food off it – shit germs climb out of knickers, you know?' I say.

'Fuck off – you're only in the door and you're ordering me about.'

'We eat off that table, you know? And you don't clean your arse properly, I've seen the skid marks on your knickers in the laundry basket.'

Gina says, 'Shut up, Morris.'

'You shut up.'

'Shut up.'

Gina shuts up. I shut up. Karen shuts up. We just do.

Karen's doing a line with a fellow she says is nice, who comes from a nice family, in a nice part of Kildare town. I think in her eyes no man will ever rate above being 'nice'.

'Terence is into karate, and, oh gosh, he has a black belt, and....'

'Terence owns a racehorse called....'

'He's going to be a surgeon like his Dad; if not, he'll be a judge like his uncle.'

She pisses me off talking about her boyfriend when Victor is out there, somewhere, facing into his second night. She just went on and on and no one listens to her. She is like the radio in the corner, voices talking away, none of us hearing a word. An annoying noise that we know we'll miss if it stops.

Terence this and Terence that; she is a Queenie Travis with two eyes, the speed at which her words flow.

Mum and Kay cook a dinner which everyone eats. It's late now. Father Pat arrives in about an hour after dinner, fiddling with his car keys, the way he does. He is all chat about the house, the rise of its walls, when he notices the extra bodies in the kitchen and asks, 'Is something wrong?'

His big face seems to cave in from the news and then he asks us to join him in a round of prayers, digging in his pocket for rosary beads.

Frank glances at Tom. They never go to Mass and rarely pray. Frank said he was in The Holy Land and the only place he got a special feeling was in Bethlehem. He doesn't know why, but it was, as for everywhere else, forget about it, merely landmarks.

Gina and Karen mumble after Father Pat, 'Our Father....'

Kay and Mum say nothing, just look at the dark windows. Me, I say my prayers at night, in bed, like I used to do to keep Dad out of my room.

The phone throbs about midnight. We are all up because none of us can sleep. Tom says he got a man in to look after the horses. He lies on the couch while Frank rests himself in the sitting-room and the rest of us sit in the kitchen, waiting for Guard Doug's long face to appear at the front door. This time he rings to say he is coming round. He says he has no news about Victor. We don't believe him.

Everyone gets up to answer the doorbell.

The guard's mouth falls open when he sees the lot of us filling the length and width of the hall. 'It's about Mike's brother.'

Mum steps into the porch and brings the door with her, but not shutting it fully. 'What about him?'

'Ned ... he's back with his mother.'

'I knew it.'

'No murder case,' he says, 'so....'

He holds a pause like it's the last warm breath of air in his body.

'What?'

'You've given no thought to filing a formal complaint against Mike…?'

'I have given it a lot of thought – no, Doug, I'd sooner not. They've been through enough. Maybe next year. It'll be down to them, whenever they feel strong enough.'

I know by the guard's silence that he suspects Mum has another reason for not traipsing Dad through the courts, but he just sighs and says, 'Okay,' and almost as an afterthought, he adds, 'Mike's left the country … went this afternoon … I didn't think he would … not with Victor missing.'

'It's the right time to leave. If anything happens to Victor he'll….'

They chat some more, then Mum says she's cold and asks the guard in for tea. She's only being polite and he knows it and is polite when he says he would love to but can't stay.

I fix Dono on Mum's cardigan at my bedroom door. It's his job to wake me up if he sniffs danger. Dono gets bad dreams. Sometimes I hear him whimpering in his sleep. I hope his dreams are about something that happened and not about to happen. I go to bed and search for sleep. Count sheep, count thistles, count Victors and count ropes that dangle from trees.

Later this morning, Victor will be facing into his third day and night in the rough. He must have the cereals eaten by now and maybe the tent up. I hope he has the tent up because the forecast is for rain, lots of rain. His torch, I wonder what'll he do if the batteries run flat in the middle of the night and he can see nothing, only hear the trees shivering in the wind and the rain plip-plopping on the canvas and the rats shuffling by the side of the tent, smelling the bits of cereal that didn't make his mouth. I hope we get to him soon. Then maybe we won't have to, maybe he'll come to us, in his own good time.

14

Frank

Grim. A grim outlook. That's all I see for Milly and her kids, a bad future. I'm sitting in the mobile drinking coffee, having just come off the phone after chatting with Fatima, thanking her for sending the MEA ticket that will fly me to Beirut this time next week, when another call comes through. I let it ring out … I just amn't ready to face the world. I get days like this.

The guards thought Mike had done away with Ned and instead found him in his mother's cottage in her mountain redoubt. The cops know Mike's form, that streak in him that lashes out, and they're aware of why Adam killed himself and have their suspicions as to who is the father of Gina's baby. When Richards called Milly outside it was to tell her about Mike. The relief flooded over the rest of us, but it leaves Victor still out there, living rough (if he's alive). Tom and I searched most of the nearby woods, helped by small groups of neighbours and guards, along with a platoon of soldiers, including some personnel from my old unit. No one was saying anything, but the searchers' eyes had begun to look towards the river.

The young fella's mind is twisted inside out. He doesn't know whether he's coming or going. I told Milly she should have got him help but she ignored me that day in her kitchen. She didn't want to know. In a way, I couldn't blame her for not wanting to know. But the cracks were showing in Victor for some time, and while on occasion they appeared to join, they were always visible in certain things he said, and in the certain way a smile broke across his face and his head nodded in answer to some self-posed question.

More coffee, black with sugar. I told Detta some time ago of my plans to settle in Lebanon. She said her husband (Fred Tex – the first I heard she'd married him) has relations there, in a place called Tyre, which I know well. She didn't wish me good luck or anything. Then we didn't part on good terms, which I suppose was only to be expected considering we weren't on good terms when we lived together. In a moment of calm spite she asked if I still had the shakes. Sam told me to be careful, and after a lull in the conversation, he started telling me all about Fred Tex riding a bucking bronco at a rodeo show and how strong he was, making me feel inadequate; then he said he loved me, and I think he said it because he knew I was hurting at not seeing him grow up, that he realised what I had long realised, that I missed him, and missing him was a constant ache. I said I'd write to him from Lebanon and give him a call when I got there. He said 'Take care'. He always says that. There was a time his sentence used to have three words but he dropped 'Dad'. I guess I don't qualify for it any more. I suppose calling two men 'Dad' isn't right in Sam's eyes.

I left Milly's this morning at about three o'clock. I needed to get away for a few hours. On the road home I experienced a sense of release. I looked forward to sleeping under my own roof and being able to pop a can without fear of reproach.

I dreamed of Lebanon. A formation of Cobra helicopters in the skies above Haddatha, their steady whine above a thicket of pine near the Muslim cemetery and the unleashing of wing rockets, leaving thick contrails in their wake and the woods alive with a burst of orange and plumes of black smoke; target engaged and exterminated. Then I saw the sun shining on the seawater, the colours of blue varying according to the switches in depths and current flows.

On the horizon, where sky met sea, a cargo ship inched to port and at my feet, the waters lapping over them so realistically that when I awoke my feet felt cold, lay the body of a young man with rope marks on his neck and a grotesque smile etched on his face, as though he had cheated someone he hated out of something precious.

Polishing off my coffee, I start for the jeep, catching the scent of kerosene from the aluminium chimney at the rear of Tom's garden and hearing the roar of the burner from its concrete cage. He keeps it on a timer because he doesn't like coming home to a cold house. He stayed with Milly last night, the whole night. I'm sure it was he who rang me this morning, the call I didn't answer, because I knew it was a call to arms, a call for the searching to begin. I don't mind the looking, it's the fear of finding something that makes me a little less than brave.

Potholes, craters large and small, filled with tea-coloured water, sign the road to Milly's. Tall hedgerows drip-dry in the early morning cold. The clouds are low, dark and roving. I think I'm out of my depth trying to help Milly; she needs so much and I have so little to give. Less, from next week, because I'll be gone. She smiled when I told her and later wished me well, saying she was happy for me. She asked me about her kids, what did I think. I said Gina's strong, is coping, but will need help. Karen's quiet but coping too. Victor I'd already told her of; and Morris, he's strong, a strong kid, but perhaps he's burying stuff, stuff that won't surface until years down the road. He needs counselling, they all need it, whether they look all right or not; behind closed doors, you know what I mean. She said I wasn't to say that, those words, from a song Mike used to sing.

Right now she needs to focus on not receiving another letter like Adam's, the one Kay burned. Kay is Milly's strength in this, and Father Pat. Sometimes other peoples' circumstances make living angels out of some people. I knew Kay before Milly did. She's doing a line with John O'Leary, whose brother I soldiered with in Lebanon. She's been going out with him for years. I think his wife knows but doesn't care, or appears not to care while it could be burning her up inside. Anyway, Kay's got life in her – she's a bubbly sort who can lift the weight from others' shoulders, by dint of sheer personality.

I'd a run-in with Father Pat before, a long time ago. I was in charge of a bearer party for an ex-soldier. He stood at the mouth of the church and refused to allow the Tricolour in, saying we were to remove the flag from the coffin. I did as he said, but only to save a scene in front of the dead man's family. I told him the next day, after the burial, when the mourners had begun to disperse, that he was a right bollocks. He put his hand to his neck as though my words had bounced off his collar.

Queenie's out, looking up and down the road. Poor old Queenie. I toot the horn and she gives me a wave. Only God knows what she's at, waiting for the fuelman or someone else, someone to nab and bring in for a chat. I drive by her a hundred yards and snatch her in the rear-view mirror. She is standing in the middle of the road, waving. I think I'm late enough as it is to reach Milly's but I pull over and then reverse, braking sedately beside her privet hedge.

'Are you all right, Queenie?' I say, getting out.

At the same time I digit the numbers on the mobile and tell Morris where I am, that I won't be too long. He says not to eat the scones. I ask if there is any word and he says, 'No.'

'Frank is it ... or Tom?' Queenie says.

'Frank.' She's in a bad way. Tall and sticklike, and half-distraught. A ship's mast beginning to buckle under a hurricane's weight.

There's no hall in Queenie's house, just a small patch where you peg your coat to a wall hook. I follow her into the kitchen, which holds a range with grease streaks marking its oven door, a pine table and heavy wooden chairs. A stairs leads to a loft, and the two bedrooms I sense are there. She laid Bob out in the sitting-room because a coffin wouldn't make a turn on the landing, not unless it was stood on its end, and no one wanted that, it wouldn't have looked right.

Queenie taps the plug of the kettle into a socket. I tell her to sit down, that I'll make the tea. I wash the grime from the inside of two mugs and only half-fill them, because she hasn't put enough water in the kettle. She slurps on her tea, now and then staring at the mug as if in awe as to how it landed in her hands.

'What were you doing on the road, Queenie?'

'Nothing ... nothing. Just looking.'

She wears a silver ring on her finger. She toys with this, turning it round and round. I can't stay with her. I need to get out and look for Victor. Milly needs to see people doing something. Even if they're getting nowhere.

Queenie sits by the fireside. She puts her mug on the tiled hearth and examines the backs of her hands – the veins are ink-blue and thick. The room reeks of damp and must. I don't like its semi-darkness; the net curtains yellowy like old eyes behind small spectacle lens. An unshaded bulb hangs from a frayed cord, alongside two lengths of sticky fly tape that have lost their spiral shape, black-spotted with fly carcasses.

'Queenie,' I say.

I remember Queenie used to smile a lot, as though she saw more amusement in the world through one eye than many others did with two.

She suffers badly from piles. I know this because I heard her arguing with another woman, saying she wasn't a pain in the hole, but had a pain there, piles of piles, so she was to get her facts right. Queenie. Mixed-up, fucked-up Queenie.

In the silence I can hear my tinnitus, ringing like crazy. It worsens when I'm tired, agitated or coming down with something.

'Queenie … that Mike Baldwin fella, he'll do the dirt on Alma again, what do you think?'

'I don't watch *Coronation Street* any more,' she says in a modulated tone.

'No … it's good, I have to say. What do you watch?'

'Nothing. I don't like the soaps any more. I'm gone off them.'

'That's a pity.'

'Frank?'

'Yeah?'

'You remember Mark?'

Mark's her son. He was killed in the car accident in which she lost her eye. I met him once. I know that because there's a picture of the two of us stuck in one of Milly's old albums.

'I don't, Queenie.'

'He was a fine boy. Bob drove too fast that day. I told him to slow down but he wouldn't.'

Queenie. I want to go but I can't leave her here with that dreadful look of worry on her face and that cancerous pallor her complexion has taken on. Let her talk it out, then she'll be fine, her thoughts exorcised for a while. Let her ramble. I only have to half-listen.

'I lost my eye in the crash. The pain, Jesus, Mary, Joseph and Saint Martin. The pain. It felt like someone had shoved a red-hot poker in my eye. Bob said I was never right after the accident. But I didn't just lose my eye, I lost Mark, and I could never have another baby. I lost three things that day, while Bob walked away with a couple of scratches. He was a big man. I shouldn't have stayed with him. He was forever hurting me, if not by car accident then with his fists, and once he head-butted me, breaking my nose. It was a new technique for him – God, my father would have – my father went off with another woman. Mother pretended not to care but I couldn't pretend, because to me it was the worse thing to have ever happened. I was eleven. I didn't know what I'd done to make him leave. I asked him to come home, and he thought my mother had put me up to asking and nothing I said could persuade him otherwise.

'We lived in Rush, and I remember Father gathering seaweed to spread on the potato crops. I remember summer and winter suns glancing off the greenhouses he kept in the big field. I remember the dry stale smell of his cacti, and tomatoes, the smell of his pipe tobacco. The empty chair the day he left, filled in the future by the male bottoms of priests and uncles, who came to see my father waked in a bed he walked away from. He drowned at sea, falling overboard on a foggy night. Bob bought this house. He wanted to live out in the country, away from the city. He was free with his hands until the cancer took a hold of him. I enjoyed watching him fade to skin and bone. I said it to him, when he no longer had the strength to hurt me. When he had to lie there and listen to me, unable to do a thing about it. He always got his painkillers but not on time. I was forgetful about things like that, when he'd to take his medication. Then he needed morphine and always more of it and that didn't work all the time, and he'd moan and groan, while I knitted and knitted and turned the radio up high, sometimes playing pop music. He hated pop music. I grew to like it.'

Silence. I take out the mobile and tot up Milly's. No answer. Shit, she'll be livid with me. But it's hard for me to face her, because I think Victor's dead, I really do. And the very notion of what it'll do to Milly is tearing me asunder.

'I like tea. I like tea with loose leaves,' Queenie says. 'They clog up the shore I know, but teabags don't hold the same taste for me at all. I heard it then, after I made the tea, a noise of feet running, running. I got up and looked through the window, seeing nothing only the black night. I put my nose to the window, and saw myself, my wizened-up little-woman self, and I didn't look for too long. Then the glass broke and a stone danced on the floor. I went out the front and checked, nothing ... and went round the gable end, because I needed to piddle – Bob never did get round to modernising the place – and I didn't like him doing his stuff in the house, because he was a bad smeller, though he gave me all the smells I missed out on when he was dying, I can tell you that. I was always afraid of the rats, but Bob wasn't. Then why would a rat be afraid of his own kind? Rats in the outside toilet, they're there, Frank, mind yourself. The security light out back throws a broad vee as far as the first apple trees. That night the moon made the trees clearer. The kids used to always rob the orchard but I didn't mind, not really. It upset Bob more than me, he never liked to give anything away, much less have it stolen on him. The wall he built came down on me one day, breaking my leg. I was lucky not to have been left with a limp. The kids were lucky it didn't fall when they were climbing or sitting there.'

She scratches her leg. 'Very lucky they were. Curses work, you know that. My mother's caught up with my father on that foggy night far out to sea and mine caught up with Bob, belatedly. And maybe his are catching up with me, now. Because since that young fella ... I haven't felt right in myself. I saw him then. I mean I saw his silhouette and when I moved closer I saw the boy, hanging. Swaying. My mind went numb and then I thought of the feet running away and I wanted to follow those feet and find out what happened. But I think I must have wanted to cut him down, because when they found me on the road I had a knife in my hand. Why didn't the stone-thrower come in and tell me? It's my eye, I bet. That Bob. He gave me a glass eye and no one could ever take to me.'

God, Queenie. What a life, I think. What a fucking life. I thought mine wasn't great. Jesus.

'And now that young fella has come back to haunt me … haunt me.'

'Haunt, Queenie?'

'He's in the orchard … I saw him … I did, with my own eye. He crossed the road this morning, carrying a stick, and then he got over the stile into the fields and sure I couldn't see him after that, with the hedges. I went out on the road hoping I'd catch someone who would see him, then they couldn't say I was mad. People are always saying that and it's not true.'

'Where did he come from, Queenie?'

She looks me over as though I am a small boy asking a silly question. Puckering her cheeks she says, 'The orchard, where else, Frank?'

'Queenie…?' I'm about to ask Queenie if she's certain but I know she's not certain about anything and hasn't been for a long time.

Queenie's lips part into an 'O' and then she says, 'You believe me, Frank, don't you?'

'Yes, yes I do, Queenie.'

She is nodding to herself as I leave. Heading for the orchard, a cool misty rain dampens my face and hair. I draw up short around the back and get my bearings: the outside toilet built of brick, a door with chewed-off ends hanging on for its dear life, lying ajar, rotting leaves carpeting the floor. The rows of apple trees, the beaten path through the middle of them, the grass thick and sopping underfoot and the smell of fruit left to rot.

Near Adam's tree I see the tent; poorly erected, sagging a little in the middle, the fly-sheet torn in places. Dropping to my hunkers, I edge forward, praying hard that Victor is asleep inside, that I can call Milly and give her some good news, for a change, from Queenie's orchard. Waddling through paper cups, cereal boxes, milk cartons and sweet wrappers, I kneel outside the zipped-up tent. The grass is soft and damp under my knees.

'Victor?'

No reply. Tugging at the zipper I look inside, catching a whiff of body odour mingling with the strong smell of a damp groundsheet. Victor is gone but at least I've found his hiding-place. I raise the zipper and leave everything *in situ*, then I head back into Queenie and ask her to keep an eye out for her guest.

She smiles and nods and says, 'An eye.'

'Yeah….'

'You see – I do have a ghost,' she says.

'No, Queenie, ghosts don't live in tents, do they, and eat Mars bars?'

'Not that little boy I had with me here the other day?'

'Who?'

'He'd a flattened nose, like a boxer's. He looked a little like Bob.'

'Morris,' I say more to myself than Milly.

Back in the jeep I try to rise Milly on the mobile but get no joy, so I slip into gear and rev away from Queenie's at high speed. I mean, where the fuck is Victor going, and what state of mind is he in, *carrying a stick,* that must be the shotgun, the one I was to take from Morris … but Morris said he'd smashed all the cartridges, so unless … unless.

15
Milly

Frank doesn't answer my call. I expect he's on his way over. Tom has gone to search the woods at Dunmurry Hill with a few neighbours and the guards are staying close to the riverbanks. I know this because Morris told me in a whisper that carried a low current of dread.

Pat's grilling waffles and sausages for breakfast and Gina and Karen are setting the table. Eric's in his high chair, while Morris is bringing in logs for the range, Dono following him. At first glance a half-normal-looking family, at second glance the worry and concern for a missing face comes through, and a third glance captures the picture in its entirety, a family waiting for something terrible to pass.

I go into the sitting-room to call Kay. She is sitting up, the sleeping bag wrapped around her shoulders, smoking. Her hair is a mess and her eyes are ring-marked and smudged from weepy blue eye-shadow. She takes the tea and says, 'thanks' through a stifled yawn.

'How are you keeping?' I ask.

'Wrecked, and you?'

'Not a wreck yet – but taking on water fast, primed to sink.'

I sit almost opposite her. Last night I told her I couldn't take much more. Honest to fuck … I just couldn't. I've reached the end of the road, run out of tarmac, nerves coming loose. The whole shebang. Kay says I must be rightly pissed off.

'As pissed off as ever.'

'He'll be fine, Milly….'

'No, Kay … even if he's alive, he'll never be fine, he'll never be the Victor he was. Neither next nor near it.'

Leaning over, I help myself to one of her cigarettes. She pulls a flame on her Zippo, and I light up, exhaling a jet of smoke.

'I'd a call from Mike,' I say.

Kay's eyebrows climb. This is news to her. We shared such a good laugh out of the idea of Ned running home to his mother. It sounded so funny. It wasn't funny when I thought about it later, but we made it funny because we were nervous and needed a laugh and fed on Ned's predicament like vultures who hadn't enjoyed a good bone of laughter for ages. Then Mike rang and I took the receiver from Gina who hadn't said a word to me or Mike.

'He has people coming to see the house and farm next week.'

'The house will be up then,' Kay says, 'most of it … Pat said some of the work can be done when you're living there.'

'Yes, I know....'

'What is it, Milly?'

'Mike told me he had a vasectomy about five years ago.'

Kay draws on her cigarette and shakes her head, picks a strand of her hair and looks at it, as if deciding its next colour, 'Surely he would have told you that before now?'

'No … there is lots he kept to himself. We used to go long spells without speaking to each other. We had a benign tolerance of each other, just.'

The significance of what I said to her dawns on Kay.

'If that's the case then … who is Eric's father?' she says.

'I don't know – Mike could be lying – he could be just saying it to hurt me, to make me go mad from the thinking about it.'

'They can reverse can't they – the operation – a friend of mine, Cathy Dunne, you know her?'

'Yeah, aha, I do.'

'Her fella got the job done in Clane, and two years later she produced a baby boy the spit of his daddy. I thought at the time she, well you know Cathy, Mrs Never Keep her Legs Together, had done the dirt on poor Paddy again, but she swore blind that she hadn't slept with anyone else, only Paddy. I asked her were we talking about her husband as there's loads of Paddys and she told me to fuck off, that I wasn't one to be talking. Anyhow, I believe her so you don't know, Milly, Mike could be lying – if he's not, then the operation could have reversed itself.'

'I don't know … I'm an expert in a different sort of ballsology. If it's neither of those, Kay, then....'

'Who?'

'Yes … who?'

'You'll find out, Milly – but don't press Gina – not yet.'

'I'll never find out. If they're anything like Mike, they'll be well able to keep a secret.'

After I had finished with the call I looked long and hard at Gina. I thought we were close, getting closer, and yet she's harbouring some dark secret. Who is this guy? Is she so frightened of him she would sooner blame her dad, because she fears him less? I don't like the way names winged uninvited into my mind. Tom, Frank, Pat … Ned … … someone we don't know, haven't met. And I feel guilty at thinking of the names that flash into my head, because these men, brothers, friend and brother-in-law, have never done me any harm. Indeed, Pat, Tom and Frank have put themselves out for me, so far out, but that's it with evil, isn't it? It lurks within good men, and tries to destroy the good they do. Tom … Frank … no … no. They're my brothers, I'd have known if they were deviates long before now. Pat … how well do I know him? Is he too good to be true? Giving me a site, fixing up a loan, building me a house, overseeing the work? Doing all this to lift a load from his conscience? Is it because of his collar that I associate him with ... I don't know what to think, who to blame, and maybe I shouldn't blame anyone except Gina, because she knows but won't say. She doesn't know the state my mind is in.

If Mike isn't the father of her baby then that means someone else abused my children.

'You got a bad draw with men,' Kay says. 'I said it to you, remember? All those years ago, that I didn't like him. He had a sneer about him but you couldn't see that. You were so blind ... then love is, isn't it?'

'Yes, I was, wasn't I? Blind.'

'At least I was lucky, Milly, the first rat I loved wanted a skinny woman with a bony arse, and the other feck I loved is married. I've long got over the hurt caused by the first and the second one so I would never let another hurt me to the same extent. Now there's....'

We say nothing for a few moments then Kay says, 'I'd love a drink, a drop of brandy. I never get the longing, but Jesus I'd....'

'I don't keep any, Kay – you know that.'

'Yes – only dreaming.' A pause. 'Didn't Mike say anything to you about Victor?'

'Not much. Nothing really, unless you call a few grunts and mumbles saying something.'

There is a commotion then, from the kitchen, sounds of chairs falling, and shouting.

Kay says, 'I bet you the grille's caught fire.'

'I better go out.'

'I'm on my way, too … as soon as I find my slippers. I have ugly toes, you know. The ugliest toes.'

Morris is grey as cloud and he grips Dono in his arms, as close to his chest as Gina holds Eric. Father Pat stands by the range, an egg lifter in his hand and shock on his heavy round face. Karen by his shoulder, while Victor, scruffy Victor, points a shotgun at them. Scruffy, smelling like a fox, wild Victor.

'Victor,' I say gently, taking in the chairs lying on their side, the broken crockery. There's a silence, apart from the throbbing of the wall clock and the sizzle of sausages on the pan, there's a cold and empty silence. We are souls in waiting.

'Victor.'

'Get over by the fucking wall, the lot of ye,' he says, wagging the shotgun.

'Vic.…'

'Shut it … shut it … don't talk to me, it's all your fucking fault Adam's dead, and—' Pat edges an inch forward. Quickly Victor aims and fires. We jump, startled by the bang, even though we expected it. Bits of ceiling plaster fall to the floor. A dark wet patch develops at the fly of Pat's tan slacks, something he isn't aware of and then is, his hands dropping a little to cover his shame. Eric cries. Terrified.

'Next time I'll blow your fucking head off.'

This isn't happening. Couldn't be. Oh God? What now?

'Where is he … where the fuck is he?'

'Your Dad isn't here, Victor, he's in England,' I say.

His head tilts left then right, as though the news is rebounding off the walls of his mind, 'Get over with the others, now.'

'Victor, I'm your mother, listen to me.'

He is agitated. His finger on the trigger, still. Jesus help us.

Pat says, his voice cracking, 'Victor, give me the shotgun, please.'

'If you fucking don't shut up....'

I follow the wave of the barrel and join the others at the wall.

Morris breathes, 'Victor, why are you mad at us – it's Dad you want.'

'I'll get him, but first I'm going to fix youse. I've been watching youse the last couple of days but every time I tried to get here … youse had search parties coming from all over the place. I thought he was here. I was told he was here – is he here, Morris?'

Morris whispers, 'Who told you?'

'You know who – yes, you do – are you Morris now … or Adam? I think you're Morris.'

'But we did nothing to you, did we? Leave us alone,' Morris says.

'Shut up – you all did something. Youse did nothing, that's what, none of youse ever spoke up for Adam. None of youse kept Dad away, none of youse.'

'Victor…' I stop. Kay is at the kitchen door, stealing forward, coming up behind Victor.

He looks at me. His eyes, I know my son's eyes and they aren't his. Misted over, distant. Don't look around, Victor, please. Don't....

Victor turns just as Kay is almost on top of him, and fires. She's blown backwards off her feet, out of her slippers. Long ugly toes. Kay lies on her back – dead? Blood pumping from her hand and face. A little bile rushes up my throat, tasting sour in my mouth. I swallow hard. Christ. Poor Kay, the warm smell of her blood. Jesus.

Frank charges in and Victor squeezes the trigger but instead of a bang there is a click and nothing more. An empty click – it freezes us. Including Victor. Frank blanches and then in a stride knocks Victor to the floor with a crashing slap to the face that drives me wild with anger.

Pat is kneeling beside Kay. Frank cracking open the barrel and checking the chamber, telling Karen to ring for an ambulance, then Gina when she doesn't move. But it's Morris who goes. Victor is lying by the side of the sofa. One side of his face pale and the other a vivid red from Frank's hand. Eyes wide open, staring at the pattern made by Kay's rivulets of blood on the lino. I sit beside him, placing my arms around him, squeezing him. There is no response. None. I could be hugging a sack of potatoes. He is so, so far gone from me. Another lost son. Lost. In that realisation I feel the tears bleed from my eyes. They come hot and heavy and for a long time. Lost.

Us

Much later, after Tom and Frank clean the blood from the floor and spray the room with air freshener, Frank says an angel must have come between him and harm.

'No ammo,' Morris mumbles, 'no ammo.'

I get my coat on and ask Gina and Karen to keep an eye on Morris, because he is shaken up a little, like the rest of us, but remember, I tell them, he's Victor's twin, and I saw the way he looked at him being led away, a look to suggest that the walls of his house had fallen down.

'And Kay?' Gina says.

'That's who I'm going to see.'

'Victor?'

'He's heavily sedated.'

'I mean, Mum, he won't ever come to live with us again, will he?'

'If … when he's better, yes. When he's better.'

There's a feeling as I follow Frank out that I've made up Gina's mind for her.

Frank eases over the cattle grids and veers left, drawing well in to the verge as cattle lumber past, driven on by an old leather-faced man wielding a stick. The sky is rich with puffy clouds and through gaps in the trees I see the red-brick buildings of the Curragh and the flag at full stretch on the Water Tower mast.

'We've come a bad road since we left the Curragh,' I say.

'You can say that, Milly, it's been bumpy, all right, that's for sure.'

237

He turns up the radio and lowers the heat. Abba's 'Dancing Queen'. He hits another digit and finds the news.

He drives on, passing the last cow, returning the wave the old man issues with his stick.

'Kay…' Frank says.

'Yes?'

'She'll be fine.'

'No, she won't ever be fine. Don't say that, Frank, because you're stuck for something to say.'

We make the hospital as the evening skies begin to close in and a slight breeze ruffles the waters of the lake outside Naas Hospital. The morgue windows are open to the last, and every dead face I've seen in this hospital: Mum's, Dad's, Grandad's, Julie's and Adam's, I see now in the grey wall Frank parks against.

'Do I need to get flowers or something?' Frank says.

'No – new hand and eye – you couldn't conjure those up, could you?'

His features pinch and I touch his elbow and say, 'I'm sorry, Frank, but one of my kids has … shot my best friend. I feel awful … she was trying to help us.'

'It's okay.…'

'And you could have been.…'

'I know. I thought about that, am thinking about it. Jesus, I've been away in war zones and this is the first time I was shot at, that someone took aim at me and squeezed a trigger. And look who it is – it turns out to be my nephew. It's a fucked-up world, Milly, and the one who caused all this, that bastard, is in England, away from it all. There's no justice. None. Jesus, the sight of his face in my mind makes me want to kill him, but I couldn't do it, Milly, when shove came to push, I wouldn't do it. And you might think it strange but I feel bad about that, I really do.'

'I'm glad you're like that, Frank, because he's brought enough of us down, without bringing you.'

The doctor says Kay lost three fingers. The sight in her right eye might return, in time. It is difficult to say at this point. She doesn't remember much, just a flash and the pain. Frank stays with Pat in the corridor, chatting to the big priest, who looks as though every votive candle in his church has been blown out.

'Can I see her?' I say.

The young Asian doctor nods. 'Yes … but not for long. She is in pain.'

Kay raises a weak smile. Her hands are out of view and a bandage covers her wounded eye. Half a mummy … something Morris might say.

'I won't ask you how you're feeling,' I say, brimming over with tears.

Her eyes have a dull sheen to them. Her good eyebrow climbs high then dives. She speaks in a low rasping voice. Heavily drugged.

'I almost got to him.'

'You were very brave, Kay.'

'I thought he wouldn't see me, but….'

The flicker of my eye, the shut and open of it when I spotted Kay, had alerted Victor.

'I left my Anusol at home – I hoped my piles wouldn't come at me – I was hoping that when Victor turned. Imagine thinking that – it's all bullshit about your life flashing in front of you, Milly.'

She joins her lips. They are dry and cracked, scum-rimmed.

'I should go, Kay, let you rest.'

'In a minute. Victor?'

'They've taken him away,' I say, letting a quietness grow between us.

'You might ring Dad and ask him to bring my cream over, will you, all my creams? God love him, I hope this doesn't mess up his heart.'

Another pinch of guilt. Her poor dad – he has yet to see Kay.

'Sure … Tom rang to say he'd bring him over … I'll remind him about the creams.'

We say nothing for moments and an awkward atmosphere presents itself.

'I'm sorry, Kay, about all of this … if you kept away from me, like some others, this wouldn't have happened.'

'Hey, real friends don't run … and Milly?'

'What?'

'Who'd think in a million years that something like this would happen?'

She says this with a smile. Then she adds that John had come in and had stood wavering at the end of the bed, like a lost prick. She told him to go home to his wife and he did, disappeared, the gobshite. 'Pat has the hots for me, you know? Though I wouldn't go down that road with a priest. Divide him; love for a woman, love for his God. Besides, he isn't that sort of man, that sort of priest. It's a pity.'

'Tell him how you feel?'

'The thing is, I don't know what I feel for him.'

'I think you do and you're afraid to take the plunge. Tell him, give him a choice.'

She gives a faint nod, eyes struggle to remain open. I know her battery has run out.

On the way home, Frank asks how she is and what the doctor had said. When I tell him he nods and says Pat is in bits, a man disturbed to his very roots.

'And you know why, don't you?'

'No, I never could see the obvious, could I? But I'm waking up to it, now.'

A week on, and our stuff is in the removal van, heading down to the house Pat says is waiting for us; brand new, as the builder's brochure depicts. None of us will be sad to see the back of the old place. One more day, one more night, in here.

The middle of November, the first bad frost of winter, the clock a minute from midnight. I'm sitting by the fire. Alone. The house quiet.

Frank's gone, he took a flight from Dublin to Heathrow and said he'd a connection from there to Beirut. He'll be back sometime. He rang from London to say goodbye to each of us. He wasn't into messy farewells. 'You know how I am,' he said. I had the feeling he was a little relieved to be putting some distance between us. I need some answers and I need them from Gina. I'm glad when she comes to me. It saves me from going to her. She cradles Eric in her arms. I don't know who that child resembles. I used to think I knew. He's awake. Last feed – there's contentment in his eyes.

'Mum,' she says, 'I have something to tell you.'

She hands Eric over to Karen who has appeared at her shoulder and we both head for the sitting-room.

16

Morris

April

We all receive counselling from Father Pat's fella. He's okay, and while he goes deep, putting you on the spot with his questions, he doesn't polish the insides of your mind the way Mum does. She has this way of letting you know she knows something, even if she's not exactly sure her finger's on the right button.

Kay seldom drops down to visit us. She wears a black patch over her eye and a fingerless glove on her hand. Behind the patch there's an eye she has to surrender soon, because its sight is gone. I hope she doesn't become the new Queenie.

She gives us a lot of smiles but they die a little quickly at times, and Mum has to cheer her up, asking how the romance is going, and women stuff like how much perfume is, and where to buy good clothes, and suggesting where to go on holiday. Mum mentions Cyprus, and places Aunt Julie used to visit – Paphos, Limassol, and Nicosia – but Kay's good eye goes small, and she says she would look sweet on the beach with an eyepatch and a glove. Wouldn't she?

Then Kay says she is getting married and Mum claps her hands and says, 'Great – that's a day out to look forward to.'

We all say, 'Great'.

'In Rome, Milly, well … we think it's better.'

Mum's features tighten up as though someone has turned a wrench on her heart.

The last time Mum looked so upset was on Christmas Day, towards evening, when we were all quiet after the dinner. No Adam, no Victor. Or Gina. This time last year they were with us and so too was the Shadow. Mum wasn't pining for him but I knew, a fool could tell, that her heart and mind were with my brothers. There was so much turkey left, Karen said – stupid like, the way thoughtless people say things.

Pat's visited a couple of times but just to check on money matters with Mum and sort out some papers. He says we've to get on with things now. Look forward, not back. I always liked him. You don't have to guard your mickey when he's around. I can imagine Victor saying that's a big plus for a priest.

Kay keeps her eye on me all the time I am in the room with them and when I tell Mum about it afterwards she says I'm imagining things but I amn't. I suppose if I were in her shoes I'd keep an eye on me too.

Us

The only good thing to come out of all this, Kay says, is that she lost three stone in weight. She says her mouth lost a supply line of three fingers and if only she had known this weight-loss secret all along. A tiny smile plays on the corner of her mouth but none of us smile back.

It's only when Kay leaves that I think to ask who she's marrying. Mum says, 'Father Pat,' as though she approves but yet at the same time doesn't. As far as I'm concerned, and Mum looked at me when I said this, isn't it better for him to change his life than to swing himself from a tree?

'Adam was sick,' Mum says, 'the real Adam wouldn't have done that.'

Mum's coming back to herself a little. It's taken a year. We had a mass in the Curragh for Adam's anniversary and later went to the cemetery, but we only stayed for a few minutes. Just because Adam wanted to be there doesn't mean the rest of us have to want the same.

I have my own room and I keep it neat and tidy, and lock up when I'm not there or at night, when I'm asleep. I trust Dono to eat the arse off a stranger, but because he knows all my family, and I know family are the ones who can hurt you the most, and Dono is on friendly terms with all my family, I lock the door.

We don't see any people we know, who know our background, and it's nice not to have them looking at us in that *way*. I'm going to a new school and have made the soccer team. The pitch isn't great, though, it's on a rise, and sometimes cows mine the place with their shitpats, so neat, round, and crusty it looks like they were built instead of dropped. But we're moving to a new pitch, a bit outside the village, and it looks to be in better condition. Victor would love this; he'd have been the star of the team.

Gina's working in Dunne's Stores in another town, not far from here. She's a supervisor now, but then she always was the bossy sort, the sort that gives the impression she has an answer for everything. She moved out on her own to a flat with Eric. She has a boyfriend too. We never see him. She never discusses him. But he exists. She has extra getting away to do. I think she's afraid of me. I can't blame her. After all, Victor's my twin, and the chips in my head could be awry or be going that way. But I don't think they are. I'm stronger than the others. I know that. I just do.

Perhaps Gina is afraid they'll let Victor out – after all, he didn't kill anyone, and they let killers out after a few years, and sometimes they get out earlier, and sometimes they don't go to prison at all, so who's to say Victor won't get out. All in all, it's a good thing for her to be gone, and a good practice for me to lock my door.

Victor doesn't know where we live. I don't even think Victor knows he's Victor. He just sits in that big sour place in Dublin, rocking on his arse, with a passing nurse stopping to wipe up the flow of spittle from his mouth. There must be something going on in his mind.

I hope he's on a desert island, with his Woman Friday, but the haunted look in his eyes, which I think have lost their blueness, tells me he's being chased by Dad, and instead of coconuts, there are Adams, loads of Adams, falling from trees.

We drove past the old house on Adam's anniversary. There's a new family living there. They have two jeeps and horses out the back. They look dead ordinary. I wonder if they've a problem with rats or if they ever did anything with the shotgun spray on the ceiling. I wonder if their daddy does things daddies shouldn't. I don't think so, but then you never know. I bet to look at our family, you'd never think it, what happened under that roof.

When Gina called Mum into the sitting-room, to tell her she wasn't coming with us to the new house, it cut Mum up a little. But she said nothing for a few moments, and then said something I couldn't make out because Karen was pulling me away from the door, telling me I shouldn't be eavesdropping. But I pushed her away a little hard and I knew by her reaction that she got a fright. She went back to Eric and left me alone.

'Who is Eric's father?' Mum said.

Shit. It sounded like it was starting all over again, when Gina first said she was pregnant and pulled some fella's name out of her mouth. A chill went up my spine and Karen was back, only this time to listen for herself.

'You know who he is – why are you asking?'

'Your....'

'You know – Jesus, Mum – do we have to talk about this? I don't want to, you know? The counsellor said I wasn't to if I didn't want to.'

'Your father had a vasectomy; so ... you know what that is?'

'Yes ... of course.'

'Well?'

'Well, fucking what – you believe him, do you? Or was it something you lovebirds, if it was a lovebirdy thing to do, made a joint decision on? That would be a rarity, wouldn't it? A Jurassic egg, you pair, doing a lovey-dovey thing.'

Silence. Jesus. I prayed Gina not to tell her. I hoped she took her bloody secret to the grave or waited until after Mum had gone to hers. She was a little too smart with Mum but Gina would know too that Mum isn't a quitter. Mum will either retreat for a day or come on stronger.

I crossed my fingers and prayed to Jesus Christ, Father in Heaven, for Mum not to wriggle out the truth. She didn't need to know, she can live without knowing, I can live without her knowing too. She's been through so much that I'm frightened. All it'll take is one more little push and Mum will just fall apart. There's no Kay, no Pat, no Frank to help her.

And Tom doesn't call round or ring. Mum has left messages on his answering machine, but he hasn't returned them. We're on our own now. Sink or swim, people have bailed out as much water from our lives as they're going to, and in a short while, even the counsellor, Hugh, is going to bow out. All we'll have left is each other and Dad's shadow hanging over our lives like a black cloud.

'Tell me, Gina?'

'I've nothing to tell you. That's not when I had to tell you – don't you care that I'm moving on…?'

'You have, oh, yes, you do have something else to say. And you bloody well know it.'

I nudged Karen to get away from the door. When Mum goes silent she's fishing for ideas, things to say, solutions; when Gina falls silent, she's about to run away.

She burst through the door, telling Mum to fuck off with herself. Our eyes met, and fell away as quickly as they'd come together.

'Gina!' Mum cried out, coming to the door. 'Someday I'll find out, someday I will, someday I'll hit you between the eyes with a name and I'll know by the look of you that I'll be spot on. Mark my words.'

'Not on my doorstep you won't. You won't be welcome. You *mark* my words!'

Gina left that afternoon, taking a ride with a fella, her boyfriend, lip-ringed and a druggie (Karen says) in a van, bringing Eric and all her stuff, to the next town. She and Mum made up a few days later, the way women do, blaming themselves for starting the row, only too happy to blame themselves for the sake of peace. But if Gina thinks Mum will never brave the question again, she's mistaken. Mum will, nothing surer. She will, and I've told her to be on her guard.

Queenie was found in a field about a week after we moved away, by a farmer out walking his greyhound. Her eyes were gone, he told reporters. I imagined the two gaping sockets, her real eye probably eaten up, and her false one only God knows where, maybe stuck in a bird's nest. I suppose it's true that a little of us lives on in some way. I used to have nightmares about Queenie, and then I stopped having them, probably because what I lived through was worse than any nightmare. Queenie just went for a walk and didn't come back, Mum said. She made Queenie's death sound *nice*. One we should all wish for.

Mum calls me in. I say I'll be in a minute. I'm busy outside, kicking a ball off the wall, trying to improve my trapping technique. Dono is barking like crazy and sometimes he puts his snout to the ball and takes it away, breaking my momentum. I go in when Mum airs my name again, lacing her tone with irritation and a little exasperation.

She sits by the range, her new hairstyle short and black, a gold rope chain round her neck, one I recognise as Aunt Julie's. Mum has tiny flesh blisters on her neck. She says they are birthmarks. I see these as I pass by, on my way to sitting across from her. I am hot and sweaty from kicking the ball. My throat itches for a drink.

'What's wrong?'

There is no sign of Karen. Dono comes in and sits down at my feet. Tongue out, eyes bright. He won't look at Mum because he knows she'll run him outdoors. Whenever she tells him to get out it sounds like she's dismissing a bad memory.

'A few things but not anything too wrong, not wrong at all in fact, depending on how you look at–'

'A few things?'

'Well, I've met someone at work. He's a nice man and he'll be calling round.'

'You thought Dad was a nice man.'

'I'm sure I haven't made the same mistake, this time.'

'Does this fella…?'

'As much as I do, yes … he knows. He was married before and has a daughter your age. I want him to know the truth, so he'll get no surprises down the road … like I did with your father.'

She tells me Gina knows, and also Karen, who isn't entirely happy that her Mum needs some warmth and attention, instead of the menu she's had recently, of shit and distraction.

'What do you think?'

'Once he keeps out of my room, I don't mind.'

I also think that this new fella might keep her mind from wanting to discover the true author of *Eric*. She'll have to live in the present with him because it won't work otherwise. Yes, the present will wrestle her thoughts from the past. Hopefully.

Mum sighs, 'I'll be inviting him over for Sunday dinner – you….'

'I won't act up.'

'Good. Just give him a chance, Morris.'

'I will.'

'Good lad – I knew you would.'

Since she started working at the new factory Mum has come on a lot – in the way she looks after herself and the way she's determined to look to the future. She must be keen on this fella, because if she wasn't she wouldn't breathe a word to him about us. Mum's face carries a slight strain.

'What else, Mum?'

'Your Dad … he's been in touch with Pat.' I say nothing. Think loads. All at once. A storm in my head. It'll pass.

'He wants to see you again, and Karen. Not Gina, though, the hatred there is too hot and I'm glad he realises that … do you want to see him?'

'No.'

'I had to ask, Morris, to give you a choice. Karen said the same, only decorating her "no" a little bit.'

'Has he seen Victor, or Adam's grave?'

'That I don't know.' After a slight pause I say, 'Just keep him away, Mum, I don't want to see him again – not unless he's lying in a coffin.'

She isn't expecting me to say what comes next. It kind of threw her head back a little. 'Will you be seeing him again?'

'Not unless I really have to … by accident.'

I sigh. That is good. Keep him away from us because he's marked us all.

'Morris? Another thing – do you know who Gina had the baby for?'

Ah. I knew this question would come, that Mum would rain it down on me someday; but expecting something to happen doesn't stop you from being caught unexpectedly.

Still, I know what to say, because my mind has been saying it often enough.

'Dad, isn't it?'

She shakes her head, her lips drawing in. Then she looks at me hard, and nods.

'You better go and have a shower." Mum doesn't talk about who was with Adam the night he died. It was me. I saw him leaving the house and later I read his letter Pat had handed Mum; she hid it in the cuckoo clock. I knew then why Victor wanted bolts on our doors, the way Gina and Karen wouldn't stay on their own with Dad, and knew why Gina and Adam had come together in some bond. Consoling each other or something, I don't know.

I was too late. He wanted to live. At the last moment he wanted to live but I couldn't keep his weight off the rope. I lifted and let him down, lifted and let him down, the pain in the small of my back hurting from the effort. He was already more than half dead by the time I got there, his kicks small ones. When I knew I'd lost the battle I cried and cried and cried, and sank to my knees, beating my fists against the ground. Then, with vomit in my throat, I went round the front and threw a stone through Queenie's window, just so she'd call up some neighbours. Walking away, stopping to vomit on the roadside, I gulped air and broke into a jog when I heard Queenie out and about. Queenie got confused about things, her mind telling her she saw Adam swaying and kicking and his nail marks on the rope where he had clawed to save himself. Heard the rope creak and felt his cold soul brush against her cheeks as it left on a breeze for the stars. Poor Queenie. I should have called in to her and told her, but I didn't want to be in the orchard, I didn't want people looking at me and saying I could have saved Adam, wishing Victor had spotted him, because Victor was brainier, stronger, and he would have saved his brother. And I didn't think to say a prayer, not one, for Adam, on his journey to wherever.

I went home and got in bed and waited for someone else to tell people.

I didn't sleep. I kept seeing Adam in front of my eyes. I kept thinking about the fun we had and then how it all changed, like a Curragh fog growing dense before you. I kept thinking that it couldn't be true what I'd seen – that Adam would come out of his room in the morning and smile. Frown, if his eyes lit on Dad.

I heard Victor turn in the bunk above me and I wanted to wake and tell him, but afterwards I was glad I hadn't, because that was his last peaceful sleep.

In the dark I lay awake, looking at my hands, knowing that they touched Adam's jeans, his Reebok